WANDERER

WANDERER

ROGER DAVENPORT

Sky Pony Press
New York

Sky Pony Press books may be purchased in bulk at special discounts for sales promotion, corporate gifts, fund-raising, or educational purposes. Special editions can also be created to specifications. For details, contact the Special Sales Department, Sky Pony Press, 307 West 36th Street, 11th Floor, New York, NY 10018, or info@skyhorsepublishing.com.

Sky Pony® is a registered trademark of Skyhorse Publishing, Inc.®, a Delaware corporation.

Visit our website at www.skyponypress.com.

10 9 8 7 6 5 4 3 2 1

Library of Congress Cataloging-in-Publication Data

Davenport, Roger, 1946-
Wanderer / Roger Davenport.
pages cm
Summary: On an environmentally devastated Earth, two teenagers from opposing social groups, the Wanderers and the City Dwellers, must work together.
ISBN 978-1-62087-541-4 (hardcover : alk. paper) [1. Survival--Fiction. 2. Science fiction.] I. Title.
PZ7.D2812Wan 2013
[Fic]--dc23
2012049142

Printed in the United States of America

To Laura

ONE

The blue-stripe was sleeping in the heat of the day with only the raised line on its back showing through the fine dry dirt, visible as a whorl of blue. Kean took note of a nearby rock before he stretched out his six-fingered hand, the one that was abnormal, and poised it above the snake. He flexed his fingers and relaxed them; breathed in, breathed out. His hand darted down and caught the blue-stripe's tail and with a throwing action cast it up, and then down, whip-cracking its head against the rock. The body was still twitching as he stuffed it into the leather sack on his belt.

He looked back to where light danced on the reflective surfaces of the big, low tent, a whole mile distant across the scrubland. They would all be asleep. Ahead the landscape became paler, more like desert terrain. Specks of quartz caught the white heat of the sun and sparkled dazzlingly. Good prospecting territory. The valley was hundreds of miles long and over three hundred and fifty miles wide, and while anywhere or everywhere there were treasures to be found just below the surface, the drier the ground, the easier it was to dig. It was not quartz or other minerals he was after; the prize find was fragments of metal, but one might also turn up other materials. It was a very long way from camp, though, and he was already well beyond the limits of safety.

Untroubled by the weight of his soft, stained leather clothing, he loped onward across the wasteland, breathing easily in a temperature of over 110 degrees and feeling sporadic movement on his thigh through the sack. The nerves and muscles in the snake's body would go on functioning for several hours.

⌒

By the time you reached the final level of education, you'd had enough of it. Feeling drowsy, Essa looked around the white-walled classroom to keep herself awake. It was a large space, yet the pyramid city of Arcone was so vast that there were those living here who had never entered it.

The Mentor spoke again. She seemed to be musing aloud, but they all knew it was a question.

"Does beauty have a purpose?"

She was a girl not much older than Essa, wearing a metal bracelet that denoted her rank as citizen. Her tunic was very short and very white. Many here wore their tunics short because of thrift; most chose a drab color that could stand a few marks on it. Essa's own tunic was a washed-out brown.

Her attention drifted while she waited for a classmate to answer the Mentor's question. Gazing through the near-opaque thermal window at her side, she could make out the angular shapes of the windmills in the grain fields. Like the great pale pyramid itself, whose white walls had faded to an ashen gray, they were made from a variety of synthetic polymeric materials. As the city's solar panels had failed one by one in the extremes of weather, the windmills had multiplied greatly and now constituted Arcone's main energy source.

A boy got to his feet. Essa knew he had sentimental feelings for the elegant Mentor and suppressed a smile. "Beauty is without purpose," he said earnestly. "We revere it for itself."

Aware of his admiration, the Mentor smiled at him. "That is so, of course. Can anyone else contribute?"

The stammerer of the class spoke: Essa's friend Veramus. "In b-b-beauty there is harmony. Harmony p-promotes g-good feeling and eff-eff-eff. Efficiency."

"Very good, Veramus." The Mentor raised her beautifully plucked eyebrows. "Anyone else? Someone else."

If someone didn't speak up they would be asked to meditate in silence for ages. Wisdom and Ethics was one of those classes that had no time limit set on it, and Essa was anxious not to miss Mania.

She stood up and said courteously, "Very often that which is beautiful is strong. Like Arcone itself, which has stood for so many centuries like a simple shape of rock, in harmony with the land, granting safety even when the great storms sweep in to assail the city walls."

Though trite, it satisfied the Mentor. Individuality in thought and character were encouraged only in theory. "Very good, Elessa. Harmony, strength, efficiency. These are the practical benefits of beauty. You express yourself pleasingly."

Predictably she moved on to debate the *absence* of beauty. Essa found herself looking out of the window again. Yes, Arcone had all you could ever need or want, but it would be nice to get outside more than once or twice a year.

∽

The long day wore on, unremittingly radiant under a cloud-less sky. Kean had wandered on to where the sand took over from the scrubland. This was not true desert like the endless expanse of the Big White hundreds of miles to the north, but unfriendly enough.

When he got back he would get sharp words from Hawkerman for his disobedience. A solitary blue-stripe wasn't much to show for it. But all was not lost: up on high, four or five gray vultures hovered, so pale in color they were barely visible against the sky. Directly beneath them something must lie dead or dying. If that something was a Wanderer and beyond help, then that person's goods would be Kean's by right if he got to him before anyone else did.

He broke into a shuffling jog-trot.

It was an albatross. Its phenomenal wingspan lay open in the most vulnerable way. Its eyes were filming as Kean reached it, and he was the last thing it saw, a young human with pale skin and gray eyes, and hair so fair it was almost silver.

When Kean was sure the bird was dead, he stroked the feathers of its neck and lifted it up. How extraordinarily light it was, for its size . . . Wanderer lore held that it was unlucky to take anything from an albatross, though Kean would have liked one long snowy feather as a keepsake from the only living thing that was capable of crossing the Big White itself.

The vultures were no lower in the sky, which surprised him; they would normally land by a victim before it had even died. He looked around carefully, reading the situation. It was his eyes that had named him. "He sees keen and long"; it had been recognized and at last he had an identity.

So, then. What was bothering the vultures? Was that tiny dark spot on the landscape a stand of acacia trees? That meant at least a modicum of water—and shade. And shade and water could mean . . .

He began to run back the way he had come. Not a trot this time but *running*, with long strides.

∽

Terrible screams rang out in the Middle Chamber, the most often used of the three immense public chambers built one above the other in the center of the Pyramid. The slightly smaller arena above this one, just below the plastics hothouse, was the Concert Hall, only used on ceremonial occasions or for public celebrations, while beneath their feet was the Measureless Chamber. In here, young people thrashed around on the white floor, squirming singly or together and shrieking at the top of their voices. Some of the sports were organized; the others were simple expressions of chaos, the only rule being that all must involve violent exertion: wrestling, Keep-Ball, Tag Two or Die.

Members of the security force, the Pacifiers, stood in pairs at intervals around the walls. For the policing of the mass hysteria of Mania, they were without the actual electric pacifors. All were large men, over twenty-five years old, with the dark star of justice stamped on their tunics. They would interfere only if blood was spilled.

Essa saw that Veramus needed looking after. Wriggling rather tamely on the floor and shouting as he was meant to, he had been swept up in a game of Keep-Ball. Three girls had stuffed the little round sack of beads down his tunic and had begun to use Veramus himself as the ball, dragging him over to others in their squad. Everywhere players were being grabbed and hurled aside, but the action was naturally fiercest around Veramus. Essa got to her feet and ran at the kidnappers, making herself into a human battering ram. The little pack of players stumbled and fell to the ground. Essa reached into Veramus's tunic, plucked out the ball, and flung it away from him. One of the girls said, "That's not fair!"

Essa scrambled to her feet. "You're not fair. Leave him alone." She was tall, with dark hair, and she looked dangerous: the girl said nothing more. When Essa walked away, she did not look back at Veramus. He would be embarrassed by her intervention.

She had caught the eye of one of the security officers. Unlike the others, he stood alone, a giant of a man whose uniform was less than spotless. His gray hair was cut close to his heavy head, and his face was bitter and scarred. It was Grollat, Commander of the Pacifiers.

The smallest twitch of his head summoned her, and she went to him.

"Name." His whisper cut easily through the tumult.

"Elessa of Bonix and also Marran."

"Ah." He looked down at her impassively. "Bonix . . . Maintenance. A citizen now."

Why wouldn't he know? Her father had some stature in Arcone these days. Still, Essa was impressed how Grollat could at once bring him to mind. "Yes," she said, wondering what she could have done wrong.

"You have courage."

Oh. That was it.

"I don't like to see people oppressed."

"Better keep your eyes on the ground then, Elessa. There's always someone who needs help." He smiled cynically. But he had not finished with her. "Would you say you have an independent spirit?"

"No. Not at all," she said quickly.

"You wouldn't say you have an independent spirit?"

"No, Commander."

"I would."

Essa could not resist the urge of her questioning nature. "What are you doing here? I'm sorry—I didn't mean—"

He was untroubled by her rudeness. "Looking. Looking for new recruits. Shame you're a girl . . . Essa."

He gestured for her to leave him. A hot flush came to Essa's cheeks, although she was warm enough already. He knew her nickname. Why?

She made herself start screaming again like all the others and ran as far away from the Commander as she could.

∽

There, at last: a flash of reflected light: the tent. But so tiny in the distance. Kean had been running for minutes. It was becoming hard to breathe. When the shrill barking came, he couldn't help but look back. A single charjaw stood, one paw raised, pointing the way to him. The others would be along soon. They should pause to rip at the albatross, but there was not enough meat on it to hold them long. How stupid he'd been; where there were vultures, you could expect charjaws to arrive sooner or later. His imagination conjured up a closer image of the creature: its huge head and balding body, the incredibly broad mouth with the curved and ragged teeth that kept the beast's mouth open at all times. Those terrible teeth that were too big even for a charjaw's skull.

It called again with more excitement, a rapid series of yelps. Kean ran on; it had seen the others and was guaranteeing them a rich feast if they hurried. Lengthening his stride, he fought to maintain a steady rhythm, one that would carry him all the way to safety without collapsing from cramps or exhaustion. Dehydration was already making him feel lightheaded.

The tent was getting nearer but he wouldn't make it. His bare feet thudded down on the hot soil, and behind him he could hear a cacophony of increasingly savage calls from the pack of charjaws. He didn't dare look around for fear of slowing even momentarily. Soon he would be able to hear their paws scuffing the dirt behind him—then the first teeth would crunch into his ankle. He would be down, rolling in the dirt like the greenback deer he had seen brought down and eaten alive. This couldn't be happening. He began to shout, but his lungs were close to exploding and all that came out was a gasping bark. The sound at least had the effect of breaking the panic which gripped him. He reached into the leather sack on his belt and threw the blue-stripe over his shoulder as he ran. A savage snarling announced that the carnivores pursuing him had been distracted by the flesh and were squabbling over it. Perhaps he had a chance, after all; his strength was renewed, and he found he was capable of sprinting. The tent was getting nearer.

So were the charjaws, enlivened by the little diversion. Now Kean had overstretched himself—he was off-balance, leaning forward, his feet struggling to keep up with his toppling body, falling . . .

He went down, rolling on bended arm so that he came up running again. Only he was no longer racing alone. Other steps tore into the earth only inches away from him. Fear brought a last burst of speed, and then he was off-balance and fell again. It saved him. The leading charjaw was already lunging at him, but its bite caught only the leather sack as they rolled in the dust together. The beast was winded by the impact of Kean's body, and he could pull himself away from its jaws. As he staggered back, falling again, Kean saw the dozen other charjaws bounding toward him. He drew his knife and swept it around. The first charjaw gave a hoarse honking cough and fell sideways. Kean had a moment to register something silver sticking out from its bald ribcage.

He turned toward the tent and reeled away from the charjaws. They piled onto their wounded companion and began to eat.

The tent was three hundred yards away, its reflective silver foil leaves dazzling under the sun. In front of it, a small dark figure raised up an object to head height and pointed it. Kean heard no noise as the weapon fired but caught the whistle in the air as another steel dart whizzed past him into the pack of charjaws.

He was down to a walking pace, limping, by the time he reached Hawkerman. The team leader said, "Come nightfall, you go and get my darts. There's three of them out there."

"You could have hit me," Kean gasped.

Hawkerman was a small man, all sinew and lean, hard muscle. His eyes were splinters of blue set in narrow slits, and his face was as dark as the near-black leather clothes he wore, the traditional broad-shouldered jacket and leggings.

He slung the compressed-air dart gun over his shoulder, looking past Kean to where the charjaws continued their cannibalism. His floppy patchwork leather Voyager hat lay beside him on the dirt where he had let it fall. He stooped to pick it up. His face under its wide brim was in complete shadow when he responded to Kean's outrage.

"Either way I was doing you a favor. You owe me."

Which was exactly what you would expect Hawkerman to say. He walked back to the entrance flap of the tent. "Since you're awake, you can watch the pot. Only came out to keep it moist."

∽

The sexes were separated in the robing rooms, where all was quiet. Women brought scented towels woven from recycled clothing and softened cornstalks. There was no wool or cotton here, only compounds of plant fiber and plastic. Like the Wanderers' leather apparel, it encouraged perspiration. After so many years on the plains, the Wanderers had adapted to the extent where water loss was minimal, but the more pallid Arconians needed to dry off after exercise. The perfumes were more a luxury than a necessity: left to its own devices, skin eventually emanated only the faintest of feral smells.

Only the highest-ranking citizens were permitted to wash in water. Essa remembered standing near the Prime Conscience, Maxamar, on the occasion when her father was elevated to citizenship. Twice a year the Arconian leader had the privilege of full immersion in the underground reservoir in a ceremony attended by the whole Council. As a consequence of this infrequent dousing, she had been conscious that he exuded a not-altogether-pleasant odor.

The ritual rub-down over, the participants in Mania dressed and returned to the Middle Chamber, where those who had inadvertently injured one another met up to exchange formal apologies. Mania itself was a cleansing process, a renewal of the spirit through physical means. After it you felt gloriously calm.

"What did the Commander w-want?"

It was Veramus. His quick, nervous smile was all the thanks she would get for saving him from a mauling.

"Just said hello."

"He always looks so dirty. He doesn't take p-pride in his appearance. Perhaps you can l-look any way you want if you're him. What's he like?"

"Kind of nice, really," Essa said casually. Inwardly her answer was, "Dangerous."

TWO

After the evening meal, families were reflective. Essa sat silently with her parents. On gaining higher status, Bonix had been given larger living quarters, though many had grumbled that with just one child, he and his wife, Marran, should have stayed in the single chamber that had housed them for so long. Essa herself would have been happy to stay there, the child within her disliking change. Their new quarters were furnished plainly, and Essa's own tiny room held only a sleeping pallet and a plastic chest for her clothes, along with one of her pictures. Marran was known as an excellent artist, and a few of her larger sculptures had been spared by the judges for long periods. When efforts at art or music notation were examined at the monthly exhibitions, most creations were deemed substandard and were recycled. Ideally a work would speak in some way of the wonder of Arcone.

The little figures Marran made from stiffened scraps of material bored Essa. They were beautifully executed, and every one of them showed a perfectly formed Arconian in a traditional pose, dancing or working. They were hardly visible tonight since Bonix, ever the good citizen, was allowing only a trickle of electricity to charge the phosphor bars on the ceiling. Only the high-ups had apartments on the outer skin of the Pyramid, and this room was windowless and always gloomy. Essa could not see the blunt features of her father, only the top of his grizzled head as he sat in meditation in front of her, tired after the day's labors.

Beside Essa, her mother was playing the bass flute. Its melancholy tones were made the more plaintive because Marran was practicing very quietly. The walls were thin throughout the living quarters, and she was considerate of their neighbors. She was rehearsing for a concert, playing the classic "The Weight of the Rain."

Essa was cold. It must be dark outside by now. Freezing. She looked forward to getting under her bed cover. The surprise she had for her father could wait till tomorrow. He was going to smile and smile.

∽

Hawkerman's team were still feasting on the contents of the pot. The vessel was made of beaten copper alloy with clasps around the middle so the lid could be tightly fixed, and it held fresh lizard and dried greenback steamed throughout the day in layers of fat and grasses, with the inevitable desiccated pulp from a desert warden. When they were not prospecting, the Wanderers slept through the day while the sun cooked their evening meal outside the tent's entrance. They trekked during the hours of darkness, unless—like tonight—Hawkerman called a "make and mend."

The trick with a tent was to have an outer surface that repelled heat. Even inside a good tent, temperatures were so high during the day that sleep was a kind of coma. The sun beat into your brain like a hammer. You breathed so shallowly you were hardly alive.

At dusk the team awoke and prepared to eat. When the temperature had gone below freezing and they were in one of the greener areas, a party would go out to gather sweepings of frost to add to the pot. Tonight Kean had gone with Ax to pick up Hawkerman's thick steel darts. Having only one arm, it was Ax who collected them, leaving Kean the more delicate task of gathering up teeth and bones and scraps of charjaw pelt. Like the Wanderers, hungry charjaws were not wasteful and had left little to take back to the tent.

There was a residue of the day's warmth still under the patchwork roof. Tapers burnt in pots of animal fat, casting cozy yellow light on the faces of the team as they ate.

"An albatross . . . I would have liked to have seen that," said Barb. She sat next to Ax. They argued passionately but were a couple. Both were strong fighters; Ax with the one massive arm and the weapon that gave him his name, and Barb with the long bow she rubbed and oiled and cherished as if it were the limb her man was missing.

Ax said gruffly through a particularly chewy mouthful of greenback, "It means the winds are starting. It wouldn't be around here without something to carry it."

"Winds must be getting strong up there, to get it this far," said Hawkerman.

"Wonder what it died of," Barb said. She was a striking-looking young woman with amber eyes and wild, matted red hair.

"Old age. They gotta die sometime." This was Wailing Joe, the oldest of the team. He looked at least a hundred. Only Kean was unmarked by the rigors of their life; the rest of them looked older than their years. Joe was in his sixties and close to being sunblind. A genius with metals, he was an instinctive engineer who had fashioned Hawkerman's powerful dart gun. If they came across the right materials again, he would make another one; a small team like this needed powerful weaponry. His name came from his memory for the old songs and legends of the Wanderer life. He made up new songs, too, as he had for the terrible drought which had killed Kean's parents when he was four years old. Kean remembered nothing of them. The drought had dispatched many who were feeble. He himself had lived because the team had taken him in and made him their own.

The other three members of Hawkerman's select band were his own partner, Cara, who was herbalist, doctor, and nurse to the group, and the mute twins Wil and Gil, whose faces were riven from nose to chin with gene faults, giving them crooked mouths and stunted tongues. Hardy warriors, they were also fine tailors, keeping the tent sun-tight and making and mending clothes with extraordinary dexterity and good humor.

Cara was very small and slight, well-suited for life on the plains, with the calm of one who is in touch with nature at a deep level. Kean had a notion that if anyone ever mistreated her, Hawkerman's first thought, for once, would not be what he might get out of the situation.

The team leader's attitude to life was not surprising when you knew his background. His father had died in a fight over ownership of a small reel of copper wire when Hawkerman was very young. In order to support his mother and younger brother, Hawkerman had learned to barter articles of value before he even knew what they were. Names were bestowed according to character and skills, and "hawker" was a term of high praise in the valley.

The Wanderers were not a fertile race, and even at the Lakes, mortality was high. Hawkerman and Cara had produced no offspring, while Ax and Barb had buried their one child, born dead, a year gone now.

Eating done, the team began the making and mending. Inevitably the terrain had taken its toll on the trailer. Light alloys might be practical, but they tended to buckle, and one of the axles needed attention.

Outside, Hawkerman and Ax wired on a reinforcement to the axle, and Wailing Joe sharpened the team's weapons, while in the tent Wil and Gil carried out essential repairs to clothing. The leather patches they used were cut from cured hides, which Cara and Barb softened by repeated beating and rolling. The noise of all these activities was loud in the darkness. Kean came out of the tent with the big pot, to scrub it clean with dirt.

"How's it going?"

Hawkerman grunted, "Nearly done."

Wailing Joe said suddenly, "Someone coming in?"

They stopped what they were doing and listened through the continuing din from the tent until Hawkerman said, "You don't hear any better than you can see."

"Sorry. I just thought, back then . . ."

He and Hawkerman went back to work. Kean took handfuls of rapidly freezing dirt and scoured the pot. Suddenly he was aware of a different sound somewhere in the rest of them. A clink of metal that had not sounded before.

"Yes—strangers," he said.

Hawkerman did not bother to stop and listen this time. He ran around to the tent entrance and darted in.

"Threat—all stand by."

Within seconds the team was armed. Long knives for the twins—the pump gun, ax, and longbow. Despite her small size, Cara hefted an aluminum spear with serrated blades at both ends. They came out of the tent fast and silent. Wil gave Wailing Joe the rusty club he favored, and the old man crept under the low trailer, a surprise package should he be needed.

"Where?" Hawkerman asked Kean.

Kean had been listening and looking the entire time. He pointed. "There for sure. Two men. More to each side, I think."

The stars shone down on a million little hollows in the terrain, causing shadows everywhere. It was hard to distinguish any life-form unless it moved. Hawkerman stepped away from the tent.

"You out there. You come forward—or do you want to get yourselves hurt bad? I will guarantee you some serious damage if you don't show yourselves *now*."

About fifty yards away, someone laughed.

"Send one into him, Hawkerman!" Ax wanted immediate and violent action. The laughter got louder. "Just aim at the noise!"

"Well, Ax," Hawkerman said calmly, "I could do that. But I just might hit him. We don't have much in common, but he is my brother."

"It's Fireface out there?"

"It is."

One of the shadows ahead of them got to its feet. "Hawkerman!"

"Yes. Come on in, if you're coming."

"Got twenty more with me. That okay?"

"Since it's you. We can't feed you."

"Don't need feeding. Be with you, brother."

∽

Two battered trailers had been pulled in next to the one belonging to Hawkerman's team, and Fireface had come into the tent to talk.

He didn't look anything like Hawkerman. He was taller, with long golden hair and a face that was alive with good humor. He wore a wonderful cloak of the finest animal skins, dyed an uneven red. It was pinned at his neck by a strange brooch crafted from brass and steel cogs, with a shard of quartz at its center. Kean had met Fireface several times at the Lakes and was impressed by his drive and persuasiveness. The raised white weal down the right side of his face was a result of a drunken brawl, in the course of which he had fallen into a fire. These days he didn't drink and had the zeal of the reformed. He got onto his favorite subject almost at once, speaking to Hawkerman but aiming his words at the rest of the team.

"The Bleachers have everything. We have nothing. It's just that simple."

Bleacher was the name given by Wanderers to the citizens of the great Pyramid.

"I got everything I need," Hawkerman said amicably.

"You do, yes. But hundreds don't. Not everyone's as capable as you are."

"Just takes practice. That's all there is to it."

"No. It takes character. If you'd just do the right thing *once* in your life, Hawkerman . . . if you joined us, with your team—well . . . more would follow."

"Nobody cares what I think. Just like I don't care what they think."

"That's where you're wrong."

"Oh yes, that's always the way with you, isn't it? You're right and I'm wrong. Should have named you 'Preacherman' these last few years."

"Wouldn't bother me one bit. At least I believe in something."

The exchange ended with the brothers smiling at each other in the warmest way.

"So . . . ," Hawkerman said. "When are you going to get yourself killed?"

"You trust every man and woman in this tent?"

"Absolutely."

Fireface hesitated and shook his head. "I still can't tell you. I got a good time planned, and it's soon. We're going to rip the Pyramid open and watch it fly away."

"How many of you now?" Wailing Joe asked.

"A hundred at the Lakes. I been out recruiting, picked up another team. We're on our way back now."

"If I were a Bleacher, I wouldn't be worried," said Ax.

Fireface spoke harder. "I don't mind my brother laughing at me. But *you*, big man—you're just a simple fool who can't see past the next meal. We're all out here dying before our time—and all we ever get from the Pyramid is their rejects, and that is plain not right."

He was looking at Wil and Gil, children of a malformed mother, expelled from the Pyramid at the age of three. The deformities so prevalent out here in the valley were the product of long-discontinued Bleacher experiments with genes. Over the last two centuries, few freaks of nature had been cast out in this way, because few occurred anymore.

"We're all rejects, one way or another," Hawkerman said mildly. "But we get by. Fireface, if you insult any member of my team again, you will leave at that moment."

"What about if one of them—any of them—wanted to come with me?"

"Oh, well. They could do that. If they wanted to."

Fireface gazed at each member of the group in turn. In his eyes was such passion and hope that Kean felt swayed for a moment. But you didn't abandon your team. Loyalty was what kept you alive out here.

"Good team," Fireface said eventually. "Pity."

"Want to bed down here?" Hawkerman asked. "We could talk some more."

"There's nothing more to say. Where you headed?"

"South."

"It's kind of late in the year. Going after your cache, brother?"

Two years ago, the team had found an area of great metal and plastic reserves in the far south. Beneath an accumulation of broken vehicles from some ancient unknown civilization, they had found unmistakable evidence that there had once been a settlement there, when the climate had been more accommodating. They had taken as much as they could carry, and trading had been wonderful at the Lakes. Hawkerman had intended to go back again for more, but events had always been against them. This time he swore they were going to make it.

He was fiddling with a bone toothpick in his mouth. Removed it to answer Fireface. "Yup."

"Gonna make it back before the Season?"

"Hope so."

"Might see you, then." Fireface got to his feet. "We're in a hurry. Do you have anything to give us? You could do that—give us something to trade with at the Lakes. There's some men whose loyalty you can buy."

"What we have, we keep," Hawkerman said from where he sat. "And you don't want any man you can buy."

Fireface grinned. It was wonderfully charismatic, that grin. "It's war—I want all I can get, any way I can get them."

He nodded to Hawkerman and left the tent.

When his band had pulled on out, the team was subdued.

"Fine man," Hawkerman said simply.

"Has he got a chance?" Barb asked. The twins turned their heads to see how Hawkerman would answer.

He sighed. "Oh sure. There's been no trouble for so long . . . He could just surprise them."

Kean said, "But you wouldn't join him."

"There's an awful lot could go wrong. And I don't join anyone, Kean. I don't owe anyone anything." There was finality in Hawkerman's voice.

Cara said suddenly, "Remember Crazy Skinner?"

Wailing Joe did. "Went missing three years back. He talked a better fight than Fireface, even."

"He went out over the Gray, didn't he?" Barb put in. "Heard some story about a big weapon lying out there someplace, went after it, and didn't make it back."

"He didn't go into the Gray. *Crazy* to do that," Wailing Joe said.

"Well, that was the story. And he *was* crazy."

"It was a story, that's all," Hawkerman said with sudden anger. "You ask me, one of his team cut his throat, took his gear, and spread the story. *That's* the way he'd have gone." He calmed down. "What does it matter? He's with the horses now, whatever happened."

"With the horses." Kean liked the romance of that phrase. It was Wanderer slang for death. The last of the horses had died over two hundred years ago; Wailing Joe had a song about them. You'd soon be with the horses if you ventured into the gray wilderness beyond the valley walls. At the northern mouth of the valley, beyond the Pyramid, was the Big White; everywhere else was gray, a wilderness of broken rock and impassable gorges. There was sickness in the Gray, too. One way or another, you did not survive long when you left the valley.

"Maybe . . . ," Kean said tentatively, "maybe he got fed up and went over the Big White."

"No. No one's done that in years." All this talk was making Hawkerman restless. "He'd have needed a Waterboy, and there hasn't been one since Little Jack, forty years ago."

"Would you have gone into the Big White if Little Jack had been on your team?" Kean asked.

"I'd have sold him." Hawkerman smiled. "Let someone else take the chance."

Bit by bit, work started up again. Kean could hear Wailing Joe humming as he sharpened Cara's spear. The tune he snuffled out through his nose was the one that was used for the song of the camel.

The legend said that way back when the horses were still alive, a man had set out across the Big White, looking for the better life that folklore said existed beyond it. He was a Waterboy, one with the gift of water divination, who could find water even in a desert. Left behind, his woman had settled in with another Wanderer after a year or so. Not very loyal of her, but as Hawkerman was always saying, "These things happen."

Then a team had gone off a little way into the Big White, where there were always stories about untold riches just waiting to be excavated, simply because it was so inhospitable. And they found the Waterboy. After two years. Recognized him from the knife he carried. People would have said he had died without getting anywhere, except his beast lay beside him. Both had been picked clean by vultures, but one thing was clear. His steed was not a horse. It was an animal with much longer legs—a bigger creature altogether. His widow had sold the bones one by one, and now no one could even guess what the animal had looked like.

THREE

"No—I'd love to—really!"

"A girl like you—you deserve to do better for yourself."

"No, it's what I want, Bonix."

In the last year of schooling, students were apprenticed to a trade. For so long Essa hadn't known what career to apply for; there were so many possibilities, so many choices. A problem with most work within the Pyramid was that you had no freedom of movement—your workplace was the same every day. Like, it would be wonderful to work in the Orchard, the big greenhouse on the top level of Arcone, where the hard angles of the Pyramid softened and curved so that the overall structure of the city was really more of a rhomboid shape than a true pyramid, and where the plastic was all semitransparent to let in light . . . But you'd be in there day in and day out until you were sick of the sight of the plants you were tending.

Just above the underground reservoir, where the workers were men only, there were the fields of plastic. A vital
and highly skilled job, no doubt, but what a dull, sterile
environment. And while it was prestigious to work on the
massive cooling system that used so much of the Pyramid's
electrical resources, the conditions were even worse. There
were an infinite number of jobs in manufacturing and recy-
cling, and all were praiseworthy—and tedious.

Once she had let slip that she would maybe like to be
a field worker, and her parents were shocked. Those who
worked in the windmills or grain fields surrounding Arcone
would inevitably—however careful they were—develop
tanned and weathered skin. It was one step away from being
one of those scavenging Wanderers, the lowest of the low in
the giant valley. Field workers never became citizens.

No, maintenance of some kind was the best option. She
had toyed with the idea of learning antiheat panel construction and repair, but not for long. The compound used
was injurious to your health, and there was no point being
awarded extra status if you didn't live long enough to enjoy
it. Often the work took place outside, dangling from a rope
on one of the four steep sides of the Pyramid. The worst of
both worlds, really.

It had come as a surprise to her when she realized that
she wouldn't mind following in her father's footsteps. Bonix
spent his days in the refurbishment of interior walls and
floors, trained in the use of the plastic mix that could cover
imperfections or tears as though they had never existed.

You went everywhere in skin maintenance. Not a glamorous job, but you traveled.

And so this morning, Bonix was smiling all over his face: his daughter wanted to follow the family trade. She couldn't resist a little lie to increase his happiness.

"I didn't tell you, but it's something I've wanted for a long time."

"Daughter!" They embraced. Maybe it was a mistake— just a whim. Done now, though. Make the best of it.

She must tell Veramus. *He* would be very disappointed in her choice.

Essa went down the corridor outside her quarters, feeling the familiar rigidity of the smooth white composite flooring under her feet. It was a feat to make the floors both light and sturdy. The secret was a sandwich construction in which the middle section was a honeycomb shape. She couldn't help but look around her with a new eye, spotting the places where the white was discolored, the first sign that repairs would be needed. The walls were less substantial, and tears often occurred. Yes, she would roam everywhere and have a degree of freedom in her job.

She found Veramus alone in one of the Writers' workshops, where sheets of black writing screed were pressed out with a ponderous mangle. After they were cut and trimmed, you could write on them with a steel stylus and white characters would appear through the black. If someone wrote a substandard composition, the flimsy tablet would be recycled. Veramus was often in here practicing his lettering, as he had elected to become a historian. Essa felt sorry for him; he would grow stooped and silent, as did all the historians after years of chronicling the wonders of life in Arcone.

"You're completely insane," Veramus said without a trace of a stutter when he learned her news. "You'll be no one."

"What are *you* aiming for—a seat on the Council?"

"No, of c-course not. But at least there'd be a chance. There's always one historian on the C-c-council. As well as the Master of the Archive—which makes two. There's n-never anyone from M-maintenance. It's a d-dead end."

"It's better than history. You're going to spend your life putting down lies in very beautiful writing."

He stood up, agitated. "Nn-nn-never say that. S-some-one might hear—don't even say that to me."

Having spoken, as so often, without considering the consequences, Essa defended herself. "I notice you don't deny it."

"It's not lies. It's a q-question of emphasis. You're en-encouraged to dwell on the g-good things—for morale."

"When we do it in class, all I know is we're not getting the whole story."

He took her arm. "Essa. I'd d-do an-anything for you. Just for me—never t-talk like that again. I don't want any-thing to happen to you."

"Don't misunderstand me, Veramus. I love Arcone. But you can't go around all the time with a silly smile on your face. It's not *perfect* here."

A smile broke through his solemn expression. "It is if you 1-look at the alternative!"

She laughed at the truth of that. For most of its enormous area, the valley was a terrible place. They were so privileged to live here.

⌒

A week later, she was a scout, Maintenance, second class. She wore a drab sash that said she had access everywhere—and she went everywhere. She wasn't supposed to; her orders were to confine herself to the upper levels only, but in practice she went everywhere because she could not resist it. Mornings were spent learning the arts of plastic patching and good procedure, and in the afternoon she explored. The scouting was ridiculously simple if you had an eye for it. You had a small tablet and you made note of where work needed doing, classified the urgency of the task, and then wrote it up when you got back to the Work Bay. However, if you missed a torn or decaying patch of wall or flooring, you were in trouble. Preserving the Pyramid was the sacred duty of all who lived in it, and for one whose actual job it was . . .

But Essa was confident and quick and made no mistakes, and at the end of every shift, she had a good hour in which to wander. After the first few days, she took to consulting the work and recreation rosters that hung in the Work Bay to ensure that she would not run into some group activity or another on these little jaunts. She took this precaution after a near-collision with the entire Council as they left the Congress Room. Maxamar himself had swept by her, exuding not only that strange half-washed odor but also a tangible charge of power and authority. He was fantastically well-muscled, and you wouldn't believe he was forty already, with his glossy brown hair and unlined features. He himself led some of the military exercises that all the able-bodied men had to attend, and it was said no man could withstand him except Grollat himself, Commander of the Pacifiers.

Essa drew back a panel to enter the Pulping Station. She had a fascination with the place. For one thing, there was the delicious sound of water—real water—as it was pumped up from the reservoir through translucent pipes to fill the three big vats. Pulping was woman's work, and so dull that not one of the workers had enough interest to ask her why she had come back here when she had already checked and reported on every visible surface only two days ago.

Stacks of paintings lay around the floor, waiting to be taken up and placed in one of the vats and stirred to pulp. This was transferred to the second vat, where it was bleached, and then the whole mess would be dried in the last vat before being reprocessed into a kind of sticky twine that ended up with the loom smiths, to be rewoven into art paper.

Essa stood in the doorway and watched as a giant picture was wrestled to its doom by three of the women. It depicted a fictional battle in which men of Arcone slaughtered some Wanderers. Essa tried to guess why the work had been condemned. It could be the expressions of bloodlust on the pale Arconian faces. Any kind of brutality is permissible in the city's defense; but don't look as though you're enjoying it. A more successful painting would have represented the defenders of culture as mournfully dignified executioners.

She watched as the picture began to break up in the vat. At the very moment of its destruction, she recognized that it was a fine work, showing the horror of man taking up arms against man. Gone now. What was the next one? A much smaller painting of a field worker blessing the sun above him with open arms. Oh.

Oh. It was her own painting, the picture she had entered in the last competition. So the judging was over. She hadn't heard. Essa felt an unidentifiable emotion stirring in her. She had entertained hopes for this picture. Technically it was the best thing she had ever produced—and it had taken *ages*. What was *wrong* with it? Absolutely nothing!

In a matter of moments, it was sinking into the darkening liquid in the vat, circling and sucked down as the women stirred with their long poles.

Essa left abruptly and went back to her quarters without continuing her wandering. In their main room, her mother was smiling to herself as she arranged the shadows by means of directing the phosphor lights onto one object or another, or adjusting burn-proof masking on the lights themselves, which were brighter than usual.

Shadow arranging? "Is someone coming to eat with us?" Essa asked.

"Oh—hello, Elessa. You're back early. Finished already?"

"Yes. Is someone coming?"

Marran went on adjusting the shadows. It was, supposedly, an art. Essa was all at once bad tempered. "I said, 'Is someone coming?'"

There was not much you could do to disturb Marran's tranquility. "No one's coming. Your father and I want to sit down and eat well with *you*. Because you are a very fine young woman, and we are proud of you. It's wonderful that you have chosen to serve in the way you have."

Essa tried to look enthusiastic. "Thank you!"

She had an urge to complain about something. About everything.

∽

The land had become very uneven: swollen and lumpy, a strong indication that prospecting was good in these parts, although daylight digs had so far brought little to the surface. So often it was a matter of chance.

Hawkerman had not encouraged the explorations; he was fixated on the cache and they were all tired, for he had driven them on at a fast pace and food was running short. Worse than that, their water was almost gone, and the familiar tensions were building. Would this be the time that their luck ran out?

Arriving at the start of a huge tract of scorched land, Kean pointed out a small herd of sun-crazed greenback deer in the early light, in that briefly pleasant time when the gigantic sun showed only its rim over the horizon before it hauled itself into the sky. Where there was meat, there should be water, too. The little deer were thirsty themselves, though: in the last stages of dehydration, when they acted crazier than ever. Generations of exposure to the sun had bred all sense out of them, and in the condition they were in now, you could lure them on by means of laying down a sheet of silver foil. They wanted to believe the shining surface was water, and they came on, jigging left and right like fidgety children. They carried their heads high, and the dry mold on their backs shone a prismatic green when the sun hit them.

Barb and Ax were the hunters. Each took a bow and bent it back. Without exchanging words, they selected the same deer as a target. You got only one shot.

At a hundred feet, the deer were wavering. As the first one jumped left and bounded off, the arrows were released and found their target. Ax hit the greenback's hindquarters, and Barb shot it full through the throat.

They packed the animal whole on the trailer; it was getting hotter by the second, and there was no time to waste. Wailing Joe took issue with Hawkerman when he heard they would be moving straight on.

"No! We gotta get out of the drylands, Hawkerman! Those greenbacks must have got water from somewhere *behind* us—"

"Sure—and they were water-crazed, and it could be two days away, and you don't have two days left in you."

"I could make it. If this territory leads into sand, we're all dead."

"That's where we're going. You go where you like."

"It's the cache, isn't it? You're so hungry for it, you'd risk all our lives to get to it quick!"

"I said we're going. You go where you like."

Of course Wailing Joe would not leave the team, and they bedded down for the day. A bad time. You wanted to be traveling, you wanted to know your fate, and instead you conserved your energy and did not even skin the deer. You lay on your back in the stifling heat under the tent's low roof, relaxing yourself into that semicomatose state.

Hawkerman was no water diviner, but he did not let panic interfere with his instincts. Halfway through the night's traveling, they came upon a grouping of desert wardens sticking up from the parched earth, those stubby pillars of cactus that were almost holy to a Wanderer. They had a taproot which reached far down, like a drill, and worked its way through rock, and miraculously drew up moisture. Working in the near-freezing conditions, the team tapped every one of the wardens, cutting into them and bleeding them into water containers. A grouping like this one would supply the team for a period of days: they were all conditioned to short rations. The great sin was to destroy a desert warden by overexploitation. Kean was too young to remember the day Hawkerman had killed the three Wanderers he had come upon slicing down a warden.

Wailing Joe was lying beside Kean. The others seemed to have dropped off.

The old man whispered, "He ain't doing right, drivin' on like this. The winds could be getting up. He said so himself. Maybe the Season's coming early this year."

It was Hawkerman who answered him, from the other side of the tent.

"Not for weeks, Joe. Never been this early. We've come this far. If I'm wrong, well"—Kean could almost hear the shrug—"we'll tie down when we have to. See it out. But we should make it back before it hits."

"Supposing we're in the sand?" Wailing Joe persisted. "You can't tie down in the sand."

"Will you leave it alone, Joe? We won't be in the sand. And the Season's not due."

"Your call," Wailing Joe remarked in a *don't say I didn't warn you* tone.

Kean also worried about Hawkerman's determination to reach the cache. It was unlike him to take risks like this. Even using the lightest metals for your trailer, a small team like this one made slow progress, and traveling more than a few miles a night was impossible. The wheeled trailer they tugged over the barren land carried all their belongings. It took time and effort.

And what if they did manage to find the cache? It would be even slower going with booty aboard. Kean would rather they turned around now and headed back up to the Lakes to dig in for the storm season. Close to the Lakes was the great pale Pyramid.

He'd thought about the Pyramid often, wondering what it would be like to live among the soft-skinned inhabitants with their easy lives and their imperious ways. When he was younger, he had fantasized about being invisible so he could go in and have a look around; now he found himself close to approving of Fireface's venture to destroy the Bleachers. He'd be an alien there because of his six fingers. He didn't really fit in anywhere when he thought about it. There were Wanderers who looked askance at him because of his unnaturally pale skin. The taxing climate out here soon marked even those who had come into the world without physical deformities.

In the evening, refreshed, they did some light prospecting. It was too late in the year to expect to find anything much. The best time for a good find was after the Season, when the fierce winds had rearranged the landscape. Then the fortunate might stumble on some near-whole machine protruding from the ground.

They worked alone, each of them scuffing foolishly at a patch of dry soil and moving on. The activity was a sop thrown to them by Hawkerman, who did not intend for them to waste too much time here.

Wailing Joe dug with the best of them, and when he called, they came running despite the temperature, for in his excited shout was a hysteria that promised something good.

Kean saw Joe bent forward where he knelt and dug. The old man's arms were deep in the loose dirt, lost from sight, and Joe leaned down even more, scrabbling away wildly.

"Joe! Back off!"

Hawkerman's command was savage in its intensity. "Get out of there!"

Wailing Joe disappeared from sight in a flurry of dust.

"Oh, that's good," Hawkerman said bitterly.

Kean saw a long yellow serpent exiting from the hole the old man had fallen into.

You could hear Joe screaming now.

FOUR

It was a whole nest of Long Ones, some dozen of them. Hawkerman pulled Joe out by the legs. The old man was still conscious, though both hands had been bitten and the venom was working fast.

"I'm sorry. I'm sorry," he kept saying.

"Thought you got wiser when you got old!" Hawkerman panted. The snakes had big heads and cold black eyes, and they continued to strike, hitting only the leather garments of the Wanderers. Ax chased and cut in half the one that had wriggled out. The others were left in their pit for the time being, along with the metal object that had attracted Joe.

At the trailer Cara said, "I don't have enough in the healing bag."

"Can we keep him with us?" Hawkerman asked.

"You know what it's like. I can't tell you."

"What I need to know is," said Hawkerman, "does he have a chance?"

"Maybe."

"Could we get him all the way to the Lakes?"

"Maybe. I've got a little sweet petal with me, and I think I can inhibit the paralysis, but to keep him alive we need concentrate."

"That's good." Hawkerman repeated the phrase savagely. "That's so *good*."

The cache would have to wait another year. The team came first, second, and third with its leader, and there was no changing that.

"Sorry. Sorry," Joe moaned. His eyes were becoming puffy and closing. "These things happen." Hawkerman turned away from him.

Ax and Kean got the booty. There were no hazards in using fire when the team was in the sands. They lit a cured greenback skin using sunlight through a lens and threw it into the den, and the serpents were smoked out and killed. From out of the small sandy cavern, Ax and Kean dragged a long metal runner from some huge vehicle. A kind of big ski with bolts still screwed into its fixings. They had seen evidence of these land runners before, but this specimen was immaculate. In other circumstances, there would have been more excavations, and celebrations for a part of the night; as it was, they were moving as soon as dusk came, headed back to the Lakes at what passed for top speed. Joe got the ultimate privilege: by now unable to move, he rode on the trailer itself as they trekked through the night.

∽

After you had learned to mix the surface-healing compound, you got to practice. Even the most maladroit could patch an imperfection if there was no penalty for leaving a rough welt where the join was made; however, the art demanded that you leave no sign of your work. Essa had somehow absorbed the skill while watching her father. She had the feel for it—the pace and urgency, the soft circular hand movements as you worked the compound while it was still pliable, the swift use of the spatula. Invisible mending was the object, and invisible mending was what she achieved.

She was working on an exercise in patching a right angle where floor met wall: the ultimate test, requiring exact strokes of the spatula. The sallow-faced chief technician came into the Work Bay and watched. "That's good, Elessa. Remarkable. But you may finish now. You have been requested to visit the Self-Examination Cells."

"Oh? Why? I don't know anyone who's been—"

"Nevertheless, your presence has been requested."

Walking along the route to the reservoir, down the sloping, winding corridors of the lower levels, Essa wondered who it was in a punishment cell that had asked to see her. No one she knew was a wrongdoer.

The corridor gave way to a tunnel at last, before it opened out into the basin beneath the Pyramid, the immense well that sustained them all. The stone walls had been carved into for decoration or practical use. There were friezes depicting moments in the history of Arcone, and different levels and walkways. You could see well below the lip of the huge reservoir, because the water level was so low. Even so, everywhere there was a silver ripple of light running along the walls . . . It was a magical place, although the demeanor of the Water Workers might make you think otherwise. They were in Contemplation of the Wonder, as they had to be when they were not active. Dotted around the rim of the reservoir, they stood with heads bowed and expressions of profound boredom. It was one of the Pacifiers who questioned Essa, asking for her name.

"Elessa, of Bonix and—"

"Ah yes. Proceed by the narrow path—to the top."

It was not a path, but steep steps leading to the highest walkway. Rough cells had been gouged into the rock face up there. Essa kept looking down as she climbed toward them, taking in the limpid stillness of the scene beneath her and feeling an uncomfortable sensation of vertigo. The steps were not wide and there was no handrail. As she got higher, cautious step by cautious step, she could see a metal cage suspended from the craggy ceiling. The cage was empty. Only those under sentence of death would be kept there.

When she had reached the very top of the steps, she walked slowly and, because of the height, slightly unsteadily down the line of cells. They had no doors; there was nowhere for a prisoner to escape to.

The enormous cavern was agreeably damp, even up here. Few of the twenty cells were occupied, and in two of them were women. None of the semivoluntary prisoners looked at Essa; they gazed down at the tiny people and the water below as they contemplated their misdeeds. One of the men lay asleep at the back of his cell. He had long hair right down to his shoulders. She wondered how long he had been there.

Veramus was in the second-to-last cell. He looked miserable and frightened.

"Veramus . . ."

"Hello, Essa. It's n-nice of you. They said I could see someone."

"I don't understand. What could *you* do that demands that you examine your conscience?"

"It's not me. It's h-history. It gets h-h-har-har . . . much more difficult."

She knelt down beside him. "Tell me about it. Veramus, I'm so sorry."

"You remember Ethics and the d-debates?"

"Yes. Really boring."

"You do much more of that s-sort of thing with history. You h-have no idea how easy it is to make a m-mistake."

"What did you say?"

"I was seeking enl-lightenment on the b-beginnings. The creation. I just asked when w-we'd learn the tales of how the Fathers built Arcone."

Other than Council members, only historians were allowed that information. No wonder they looked self-important. Maybe it was the weight of their knowledge that made them so stooped.

"So? What happened then?" Essa asked.

"They said an a-acolyte d-doesn't ask that qu-question. He w-waits to be t-told at the p-proper time. And then I was s-sent here."

"What?" Essa couldn't believe it.

"A-apparently there's always s-someone who asks th-that. Th-they're waiting for it. It w-would be me, though. S-seat on the Council? I can forget *that* now!"

Essa tried to comfort him, but he wanted her there only so that he could have someone to complain to about the unfairness of it. He was still inconsolable when she left him. He would be in the cells only a matter of days, but the stigma would be with him for the rest of his life.

It made you wonder—wonder about how you were taught to be so grateful for the protection of the Pyramid that you shouldn't question anything. It would be something to find out how it all started, wouldn't it? Well . . . wouldn't it?

If, that is, you could.

～

They were traveling during the first and last hours of daylight as well as at night. Cara strayed from the trailer to search for plants and roots with which to replenish her healing bag. Often Kean went with her, putting his sharp eyes to use. At night he was a moisture gatherer, in charge of the laborious process of setting water traps with sheets of plastic. In the right conditions, a half-buried sheet of plastic collected water by way of condensation. Each morning when the sun had warmed the ground sufficiently, he inspected his traps and siphoned their pitiful contents into a water bag. Then he would lope after the team and add his weight to the human engine that propelled the trailer.

The wells and waterholes were few and far between, and dried up. Except for Kean, who never burned, they were all suffering terribly as skin flaked and peeled from their darkened, desiccated faces. Wailing Joe was so ill it was hard to tell if he still lived.

After two weeks, Hawkerman forced them to begin traveling from midafternoon onward. With the Season approaching, the temperature had become bearable.

A few days in, they came across the Cruisers.

∽

It happened at a moment when their hearts had been lifted by a sight to gladden any Wanderer's eye. In the last of the day's light, Kean spotted a low dark smear on the horizon that was undoubtedly a large stand of acacia trees. As they came nearer, the size of the fertile area raised their spirits further. There would be water there. Soon the detail of the low-standing trees would be revealed to them: the greedy stretching of the twisting branches, the little tattered double leaves.

As the sun set behind the trees, it seemed they could see the sparkle of water somewhere among them, although it was difficult even for Kean to make out much against the reddening sky.

When he was sure, he said, "It's occupied."

"Or is it water?" Hawkerman said, squinting.

"It's metal. Above ground level."

The team leader accepted Kean's judgment without question. His own sight was good for a Wanderer, but not that good. "Tents? It's reflectors, right?"

"Vehicles. Two or three. Big."

Hawkerman ran a dry tongue over dry lips and swore, something he hardly ever did. "Cruisers," he breathed grimly.

Ax said, "It wouldn't be Cruisers. Not so far south."

"It shouldn't be, but it is."

"What we going to do?"

"The light's coming our way. They've seen us for sure."

"Can we go around them?" Ax asked.

"Not if they don't want us to. And we need the water, any case."

Even Barb was apprehensive. "Maybe they've taken all the water already—for the vehicles. We should backtrack right now. It'll be dark in no time."

"If we show we're avoiding them, it's going to give the wrong signal, and they'll come after us. No one to stop them and no one to see—what do you think's going to happen?"

"Go on in, then?" Kean asked with a grimace.

"Yup. Just like everything's fine and we got nothing to worry about."

Those who had not expressed doubt were those who followed Hawkerman with the greatest love and loyalty: Cara and the split-featured twins. Even they looked somber as the team hauled the trailer toward the trees.

A fire was being built in the largest clearing among the low-sprawling trees. It increased the sense of threat they all felt.

The sun had dropped from sight, and blue night had come by the time they were close enough to make out the figures of men in the clearing, where flames had begun to roar up through the dried leaves on the trees. No one acknowledged their approach, but they knew they were being watched.

"Shouldn't we have put someone in with Joe, undercover?" Ax whispered. He and Hawkerman were at the front of the trailer, pulling it.

"Need to show all the strength we can."

Kean thought, *What strength?* There must be thirty men there, and every one a Cruiser. Their jerkins and leggings gleamed with the flashy metal ornaments they affected, which were worn only partly for show; they also comprised a rough kind of armor. Pieces of beaten steel, machine parts— any oddments of metal that could be stitched to leather, the more bizarre the better. They wore caps of beaten metal on their heads, and their elbows and boots were steel-capped, too. You never had any doubts as to when you were with a Cruiser, and when you were, you knew that you were in the company of a man whose chief characteristic was brutality.

Kean felt nervous to the point where his legs were shaky. You hardly ever saw Cruisers away from the Lakes, and it was almost unheard of for them to be traveling in such numbers—using three vehicles! The machines were long and low and light, from thirty to sixty feet in length, crafted from aluminum panels and running on spindly wheels of great radius. The engines were antiques and copies of antiques, and if you ever dug up a machine part for one, well, the exchange you could make for it was fabulous. Hawkerman's team had a piston rod stowed somewhere in the trailer. Kean wondered if they would have to trade it for their lives.

Hawkerman let go of the leather strap attached to the trailer. He said to the twins, "Haul it to the other side of the trees, not too close. Be ready to move; if anyone comes toward you, obey the usual rules."

It didn't matter if you were smiling warmly with outstretched hand; out here if you got within a few yards of someone's trailer, you had to be invited to step nearer or blood was shed.

The twins nodded and the team split up, with Hawkerman leading the others into the sprawling mass of acacia trees.

"Well! It's old Hawkerman!"

A man stepped from behind one of the leaning tree trunks. At once others materialized in a similar fashion. Beyond them the fire crackled savagely. Particles of hot ash flew straight upward in the windless night.

"Snakebite. You're a long way from home."

"Last chance to see anything before the Season."

Kean had come across Snakebite before, at the Lakes. He was tall, stringy, and mean, and he liked an audience when he used his knife. There was something snakelike about his pebble eyes, and he was wearing his famous broad belt of rare reptile skins, studded with their own teeth.

"And have you?" Hawkerman inquired politely, after holding Snakebite's eye for a length of time he made deliberately uncomfortable.

"Have I what?" Snakebite kept smiling.

"Seen anything?"

"Not a living thing. Till we saw you." The smile died away. "You come on in." The traditional invitation.

"Happy to," Hawkerman said. "Our thanks." And he walked past Snakebite toward the fire.

No turning back, not now. Kean and the others followed him. Kean smiled at Snakebite as he passed, keeping his eyes steady and fearless as he did so.

He wished his legs were working better.

They gazed around covertly as they walked to the fire. The Cruisers had not been delicate about feeding the blaze, and whole branches had been ripped from the trees at random. Kean saw Hawkerman's mouth tighten; no Wanderer would commit such an act of despoliation. Where the environment was friendly, you encouraged it to remain your ally.

When they reached the bonfire, Snakebite waved away those who had come back to warm themselves by its heat. It was already getting very chilly. Kean saw that the Cruisers did not go far; they took up stations between the nearest trees, preventing any rapid exit from the clearing, keeping their hands close to the weapons in their belts. Metal gleamed on them at every point. Flight was impossible now the "guests" had got this far in among the low, crooked branches.

"So what's your situation?" Snakebite asked.

Hawkerman played it straight. "Got a sick man with us. We're hurrying for the Lakes. Need some sweet petal concentrate."

"Sorry we can't help you with that. And you need water?"

"If you've left any after feeding them." Hawkerman nodded toward the vehicles.

"There's some. We been rolling by hand these last nights. Needed all the water we could find here."

A little hint of sarcasm: "And you've been seeing the sights, have you?"

"No, no." Snakebite smiled. "No—I had this notion to do some prospecting on my own account. Seems like I been paying for goods all my life when I could just pick them up like you people do."

"Found much?"

"Found it's hard. Going to leave it alone, here on in."

"Well, we won't bother you. Just fill up our water skins and move on."

"What about you? Loaded with gear to trade, I guess?"

"Some. I'll do my trading at the Lakes."

"I could offer a fair price here and now—save you the trouble."

Hawkerman stared at Snakebite. Cara and Ax looked calm and relaxed; Barb was on edge and fingering her belt near the handle of her knife. Seeing Hawkerman's stare, Kean discovered his legs had stopped shaking. Something was going to happen and he had to be ready.

FIVE

Kean caught Barb's eye, glanced at her knife, and moved his head in a near-invisible warning that she was showing stress. Her hand dropped down.

Snakebite was getting irritated. He tried to keep it in. "'Hawkerman.' That's what they call you. You're a trader—why not show us what you got to trade?"

Hawkerman was equable. "I told you what I'm going to do. Where's the water?"

Snakebite led them through the trees around the back of the motorized wagons. The well had been cared for over the years; now the rocks covering it were lying strewn around haphazardly. Hawkerman climbed over them and looked down as far as he could in the darkness.

"There's water—it's just a long way down now," Snakebite reassured him.

"Way, way down," Hawkerman said and stood back from the well. "You certainly have tried to drain this."

"You want some or not?"

"I don't like to see the trees cut up too much," Hawkerman mused. He asked politely, "You know anything about them?"

"The wood's good for fires." Snakebite laughed.

"That all you know?"

"Don't be dumb. I know it's good hard wood, and a man can make things out of it. What is this—you think I'm stupid?"

"Did you know that you can get an acid from the nuts of these trees, and it's good for burns? Sounds strange: it's true. Did you know you can get remedies for some fevers from these trees?"

"No, I didn't. You want to shut up now?"

Hawkerman went on relating his interesting facts. "Did you know you can eat the seeds? And that you can boil glue out of the gum these trees produce?"

"No. You finished?"

"Well, there's more, but since you're not interested, let's move on to the water. It looks like this was a pretty good well before you got to it. Taking so much from it . . . that's a bad idea, Snakebite."

Now he sounded deadly serious. Kean knew the thing that made Hawkerman the angriest about the Cruisers was that the engines of their vehicles were water powered. It was the ultimate in waste as far as he was concerned.

"You want water, Hawkerman?" Snakebite demanded bluntly.

"Can't live without it."

The Cruiser persisted, "And you want some?"

"Yes."

"So, trade," the cold-eyed man directed.

Hawkerman smiled, easy and calm. "We don't trade for water out here."

"See, Hawkerman—we were here first. So it's like at the Lakes."

Ax spoke up, "We don't do it like that. You're not at the Lakes—you're in the outlands, and things work different."

"Seems to me it's just the same, big man. And there aren't that many of you, when all's said and done. I don't want to come out into this hell and go back with nothing. So show us what you got in the trailer, or I'll just take a look myself, and price it myself, too."

Ax's muscles started to bunch. Hawkerman put a hand on his back, relaxing him. "Well . . . we're in a hurry. Maybe sometimes you do have to break with custom."

Snakebite smiled in open triumph. "That's better. So let's take a look in the trailer."

Hawkerman looked tired and beaten. "We could do with a drink right here and now. We can sort through the goods later and set prices. But I need a drink. Don't worry—we'll pay." He spread his arms wide. "You see anything right here that you like?"

As Hawkerman turned toward Kean, Cara, Ax, and Barb, indicating them and the things they carried, the pump gun strapped to his back was right in Snakebite's line of vision. It was by far the most valuable thing on view.

Snakebite said at once, "I'll take the shooter."

"Oh, come on! Not that! Just for a drink of water?"

"We'll work it into the whole deal, don't worry. Now, are you going to trade, or are we going to have a very bad disagreement?"

Hawkerman unstrapped the gun slowly and sadly, showing no threat in his careful actions. He sounded subdued, depressed. "You know how to work the lever?"

"'Course I do."

"It's powerfully stiff. You have to be strong."

He handed the gun over. Snakebite took it with glee and began to demonstrate how easily he could unclip the lever and force it down. The next moment, his hands full, he found his own curved knife at his throat, whipped from his belt by Hawkerman. At the same instant, the four team members drew their own knives and formed a defensive circle around the two men. Kean had known that the one thing Hawkerman would never part with was his gun, and the thought of possessing it had left Snakebite vulnerable.

"Yes, Hawkerman is my name," he whispered into Snakebite's ear, "and I do trade. And you are what I'm trading."

A couple of the Cruisers took a step forward, and then the whole of the encampment was still.

"You can't do this!" Snakebite was livid, his eyes wide open in fury and frustration.

"You all stand back!" Hawkerman commanded the Cruisers. "I was telling your top man here about how we do things away from the Lakes. We do not empty wells or rip down trees. You did wrong." He lowered his voice. "Snakebite, I'm going to borrow your three Cruiser wagons. You will steer one, and I'll take two of your men to drive the others. I will kill you where you stand, otherwise—my word on it."

Snakebite hesitated as rapid thoughts ran behind his reptilian eyes. They did not appear to comfort him. Hawkerman had a reputation.

∽

Snakebite was rigid with humiliation and rage as he drove the battle wagon. Hawkerman stood balanced right behind him, holding the curved knife to his back. The vehicle rocked and swayed as they rattled over the cold ground, and Kean began to enjoy the new experience. In the rear, Cara held onto Wailing Joe, trying to keep him from rolling around. The team's trailer jounced along behind, lashed to the wagon with braided leather ropes, and the other two wagons traveled on either side of them. With air whistling through the visor slit, it was freezing in the long functional cabin. The interior was lined with cream-colored synthetic insulating pads, giving it a somehow domestic feel.

∽

As dawn came up, the engine began to splutter for lack of fuel.

"See?" Snakebite croaked, stiff and tired. "You been taking it too fast."

"Sure. Pull up right now," Hawkerman said.

Snakebite halted the wagon carefully. "Now what?"

"Well . . . my thanks," Hawkerman said amiably. "You've been most helpful. "Now we're all going to camp down here till dusk. You and your two friends as well."

No one slept much in the tent. Kean was very aware of Snakebite and the two other Cruisers, tied up within four feet of him and taut with resentment.

It was still light when they packed up the trailer and went back to being Wanderers. First they siphoned off what little remained of the water in the battle wagons' fuel tanks. Kean and Ax were the ones with the duty of transforming the tent back into the trailer and getting the comatose Joe settled on it and undercover. Cara was with them, worrying about her patient.

When Kean looked for Hawkerman, the team leader was jumping down from the biggest battle wagon. He was carrying Snakebite's belt. As Hawkerman walked to the trailer, Barb and the twins hustled the two other Cruisers into the wagon. Kean saw there was a bruise coming up on Hawkerman's cheek, showing dull red on the dark skin.

Kean said, "You took his belt."

"Yes. He needed some persuading, but I made him see reason. I put it to him that he wanted to trade my gun for some water that wasn't there, so it seemed only just and proper to trade his belt for some goodwill that wasn't there."

"You've made an enemy."

"Kean, I did that already. I'd rather he was dead, but I can't afford to put myself in the wrong."

Later, Kean was paired with Barb, pushing the trailer from behind as the team toiled over the brown earth. He panted, "So what happens with the Cruisers?"

She gasped back, "Hawkerman left them three days' water . . . the others knew where we were headed . . . if they got any sense of direction, they'll catch up in a day or two. Then we just hope they don't find the water to fuel up and come after us."

"Well . . . we saved some time, anyway. Might even get to the Lakes for the Face-Off."

"Wouldn't think so. Who cares, anyway?"

Kean did. The annual Face-Off was the one time you got to see Bleachers: real, unblemished Bleachers, so provokingly clean and contemptuous.

⤳

Now she was an apprentice, Essa had the privilege of attending The Day of Offering, where they would come face to face with Wanderers. She was excited as her mother fussed over her. Marran had stitched together a new cream-colored tunic for her daughter and was twitching at it so it hung just so.

"Your old one will do for work, and there's the blue one where the material is discolored, too . . . Did a girl ever have so many clothes as you?"

"This one is perfect. Thank you, Marran."

Bonix was waiting for them in the corridor, and they joined the steady stream of citizens and residents filtering down to the main entrance. All were solemn-faced, correctly hiding their pleasure at the forthcoming excursion from Arcone. In the giant lobby stood the impressive plastic figures of bygone rulers of the Pyramid. You could see how the manufacture of these had improved significantly over two centuries, with the most striking statue of all portraying Maxamar's predecessor as Prime Conscience, Pillat the Benign. He did not look benign at all; the stern expression demanded respect. For what, exactly, it would be hard to say. His period in office had been entirely uneventful.

The broad doors had been winched up high and sunlight streamed in, blinding the orderly lines as they shuffled out slowly into a yellow heat haze so bright the figures were lost to sight like souls vanishing into heaven.

Essa felt the sun slam into her as she came out through the stately portal with her family. Sweat started from her forehead at once. Pacifiers lined the dirt road through the recently harvested fields, carrying the long gray cylinders which gave them their name, with power packs strapped on behind. They directed the population to designated viewpoints according to rank.

Those who were residents of low standing were not allowed past the ring of windmills. Entitled, as a citizen, to a position in the front ranks of the spectators, Bonix had a word with one of the Pacifiers, and he, Marran, and Essa left the road and trudged through the sharp grain stalks, under the motionless sails of the windmills, to join other senior maintenance workers and construction engineers at the very edge of the perimeter ditch.

Essa took it all in with an excitement that used up energy at a rapid rate. Over to their left stood a group of bakers, and immediately on their right was a line of electricians. Beyond them the podium had been erected for the Council. The leaders of Arcone lined the steps already, with a fifty-strong guard around them. On the pure white of the topmost step, Maxamar stood alone, as unmoving as his statue in the lobby would be when he himself was dead and gone. Just below him was Grollat, arms folded, looking out over the flatlands of the valley.

What a sight it must present, this annual demonstration of the power and order of the civilized people of Arcone. Rows of defenders of the Pure Life, dressed in tunics that were almost uniformly pale in color because dye was so expensive; and each trained to one degree or another in martial skills. Behind them, the simple grandeur of the ashen Pyramid itself.

Essa saw Grollat raise a hand to shade his face, and she looked out at the valley again, following his gaze. They always came from the scrubland, never from the sands of the Big White, which began on the other side of the Pyramid at the valley's entrance. They marched or drove from the Lakes. Was it a day of festival for the Wanderers, as it was for the Arconians? Or was it only age-old antagonism and bitter curiosity that brought them here? She had never asked.

Yes, there was a dribble of mankind approaching. She shuddered in happy anticipation of seeing the scavengers up close. Filthy, horrible, and ignorant they would be, without ethics, morals, or even enough plain common sense to keep them from springing at your throat if they had the chance. The only controlling factor was fear: fear of retribution from Arcone.

Suddenly there were hundreds of them, coming from the whole sweep of the horizon. Shambling bunches of sun-ravaged humanity, looking bigger than they really could be, because of their absurd clothes made from the skins of animals. And now there was a glittering series of reflections off metal, and a clattering, throaty sound. Cruiser wagons, racing through what was fast becoming a multitude, scattering it, heedless of danger to those on foot. The vehicles *did* look dangerous, in a primitive kind of way. They each came to a halt in the same fashion, in a showy broadside that threw up dirt in a kind of sneering defiance. They disgorged their human Cruiser content like little tin boxes dropping quantities of shiny-backed beetles; the metal ornamentation on these warlike creatures glinted in the sun.

The Wanderers kept coming. Cruisers and walkers alike, all stopped at a distance of at least three hundred yards from the outer ditch where Essa stood, glad now to be among so many of her own kind, yet sorry to be so far away that she could not see the features of the vagrants. Some of them were horribly deformed, she had been told, and it was a shame one couldn't get the full thrill of this encounter between the races. Gathered outside Arcone today would be nearly every living person in the valley. Surely never anywhere else in history had such a host come together!

"Ah. At last," Bonix said beside her. The business of the day had begun. Two Pacifiers had lifted up a basket woven of plastic and were setting out toward the alien nation opposite. A bunch of shining hothouse tomatoes topped the cornucopia of temptations inside the basket. There would be other foodstuffs in there, and paintings and musical instruments, as well as the single short-barreled pacifor which was offered every year. It would even work—for a while, until its power supply was drained.

The Pacifiers bore the basket to a point midway between the opposing assemblies and set it down on the dry earth. Their courage was laudable; they set off back to their own lines at a dignified pace without once looking behind them to where the Cruisers revved their engines threateningly.

"Marvelous," Bonix announced to no one in particular.

But a little boring, too? Now the Arconians would wait for some minutes before the Pacifiers retrieved the basket, which would remain untouched by scavenger hands. Essa fidgeted and looked across at Maxamar. He had not moved an inch.

A collective gasp came from the Arconians whose view of the scene was not obstructed—a single Wanderer was running out to collect the basket.

He ran awkwardly in his leather clothes, which must be stifling hot. He must also be—surely—under the influence of fermented substances. It had been years since any Wanderer had taken up the challenge. Now Maxamar moved. He fidgeted from foot to foot on the podium before catching himself and resuming his autocratic pose.

Grollat was walking slowly down to the foremost Pacifiers. He strolled along the line and stopped. Placed his hand on a man's shoulder. The Pacifier stepped forward and unslung the weapon he carried. Grollat spoke to him quietly, and the officer adjusted the two switches near the trigger.

The Wanderer was staggering forward as he ran. The Pacifier set his feet wide apart for balance and aimed. The jagged electric bolt, silver blue and the size of a handball, tore through the air and flew past the Wanderer, dropping well short of the others of his kind. The Pacifier set his feet yet again and waited a moment, allowing his target to reel closer to the basket. He fired again and suddenly the Wanderer was farther away from his objective, hurled ten yards backward at a speed he had never experienced before and was not experiencing now, because he was dead.

Essa's mind went empty. She felt a constriction in her throat and stomach. This was not what should happen, a man killed because just once in his life he wanted a taste of the better things in life. A man who certainly could not have been thinking of the consequences of his action. The way he had run—it was desperation of some kind, not defiance.

All the Pacifiers had their weapons at the ready as their two comrades marched out to retrieve the basket.

There was no more trouble. The basket of temptations returned, the Council came down from the podium and went back into Arcone. Essa stood where she was until her father physically turned her around toward the Pyramid.

"Had to be done," he muttered uneasily.

The outlanders were leaving the scene, too. Three of them stayed to reclaim the body.

SIX

Kean missed the Face-Off by a couple days. Nearing the Lakes, they came across a solitary water seller who related to them the tale of the murder. Had they arrived a few weeks earlier, there would have been others like him to pester them from the stalls they set up at a distance of around ten miles from the Lakes. As returning teams struggled in, the sellers hoped to encounter one so desperate it would pay top price for a small skin of water.

Hawkerman said, "Got some Cruisers coming in soon—maybe they'll be in need."

The water seller blenched. "Cruisers?"

"Three wagons full. All of them thirsty. Didn't seem to know the ways of the flatlands."

"Don't move on—I'll come in with you."

Hawkerman smiled at the man's haste. "That will cost you two skins."

"What? Oh . . . yes. One skin."

"Two."

"Two if we see them."

"Okay."

Hawkerman held out his hand and the man shook it reluctantly. "You're sure you're telling the truth about the Cruisers?"

"You say I'm not?"

"No." The man sighed. "I'd like the company, anyway. Going crazy out here by myself."

It took one more night to make the journey, and the water seller joined them in the tent while they ate. He had his own dried charjaw tablets. He'd heard nothing about Fireface coming in yet. Hawkerman guessed that his brother was still on his quest for recruits. That was when they learned that the man who had been killed at the Face-Off was one of Fireface's followers, a young man who was drunk and wanted to inspire others.

"Why would he want to do that?" Kean asked, hitting a note of absentminded query he had picked up from Hawkerman. It got people to talk to you.

The water seller said, "Well . . . Fireface . . . well . . . there were a lot prepared to listen to him, but only when he was around, see? This young buck wants to get them worked up again—for Fireface. That's the story."

"And it didn't work," Hawkerman said.

"Well, hardly. The reverse, you could say. But he got all the attention he wanted . . . for a minute."

⌢

Kean always had a sensation of returning home when he came to the Lakes. The ground slowly dipped into a shallow bowl in which the soil was almost fertile enough to grow crops. Almost but not quite. Giant acacias were scattered everywhere, providing welcome shade. You traveled under them from light to shadow and back again. The poorest Lakesiders lived on the outskirts of the sprawling settlement, in derelict tents or covered dugouts. Farther in, the tents became more substantial and the trees even bigger and grouped closer together. Here you could hire yourself a patch of ground on which to see out the Season; the tree cover and the basin itself provided a natural windbreak.

Needless to say, there was not a lake in sight. At the center you could see the broad hollows marking the lowest points of what must once have been a single great expanse of inland water; now they resembled craters more than anything else, and a variety of gray lichens grew in them. The water was here, in deep-sunk wells, and it was by the water that the Cruisers lived in the semipermanent shacks they favored, which doubled as trading posts.

The Lakes were where all the bartering and dickering and hawking and haggling went on, and through organization and brute strength, the Cruisers had come to control the whole of the site. Local knowledge had it that beneath the valley floor was a formation of impermeable rock which channeled the yearly downpours to this end of the valley. Beyond the Lakes, the Bleachers had the very best of it; here were only nature's leavings. The largest well of all was the oldest, with a ragged rim of boulders around its twenty-yard circumference. Beside it stood the only two-story dwelling, a sagging, fully wooden structure, and in that dwelling sat Dagman, the dominant Cruiser. He never came out of his shack, and controlled his interests through a network of spies and subordinates.

When Kean had once asked Hawkerman's opinion on Cruisers, he had felt somehow disappointed in the team leader, who had said, "There has to be order somewhere. Who do you think is going to control things? The storytellers? Someone has to regulate the water and the trading."

Kean had said, "But it's not right, them having the best of everything."

"Did I say it was right? I didn't say it was right. I said someone had to do it. Otherwise there'd be even more fighting and killing and bickering than there is, and the wells would run out before time. And you know, Kean, if it wasn't the Cruisers, it'd be people just like them only wearing less metal. Got to have someone strong in charge. Things don't function otherwise."

They hired their ground at a spot under a single big tree. Not the best cover, but where there were too many trees, some thief was likely to sneak up on you. The Cruiser who ran the little site allowed himself to be paid in plastic articles only: he knew it was better to take full payment in advance than promises of steel or aluminum. There was no guarantee the debtor would live to pay. The richer Cruisers accepted labor as payment—preferred it, even, for the sensation of power it gave them.

Before he left their new camp, taking Kean with him, Hawkerman directed Cara as to which articles she should use for bartering for immediate necessities, including the medicine for Wailing Joe. The old man had stabilized to a condition where, though paralyzed, he could take water. He was thin as a stick and weighed nothing at all. "He'll make it," Cara told Hawkerman. "Seen them worse than that and still make it through."

Hawkerman said, "Got to fix it so we all make it. Back in a while." He gave his gun to her, and he and Kean walked away through the trees, heading for the middle of the Wanderer settlement. Hawkerman carried a bag with him. It didn't look very full, if they were going to trade.

"Where are we going?" Kean asked.

"Dagman. You're here to watch our backs. Take my signals."

"Yes," Kean said, hiding the nervousness that had hit him.

The farther in you got, wending your way between the tents and dwellings, the more Cruisers there were. Beside every battle wagon stood a single guard. Beside one wagon there was no guard, since it had been transformed into a stationary caravan. It was a solar-powered vehicle, now burnt out. No one knew how to fix those things anymore. Here a Wanderer and his son were dragging a barrel on wheels, bringing back water they had bought. Hawkerman stepped to one side to let them use the narrow path they were on.

"Thanks," the man said. "Hey—do I know you?"

Hawkerman said nothing in reply. The limit of his courtesy had been reached when he made way for them to pass. The man's frown cleared. "Hawkerman—it's Hawkerman, isn't it?"

"Yes."

"You got any room in your team for my boy? I'm looking to place him."

"Sorry—no room."

"I'd make it worth your while."

It was common practice for families to apprentice their children to the top teams in return for goods. Hawkerman did not give the offer a second thought.

"I said no room."

"Oh. That's a pity. Sorry to trouble you."

Hawkerman smiled politely. The boy kept his head down, and Kean was sure he was blushing. The father added to his son's mortification by continuing the conversation. "Where you off to? Trading?"

Hawkerman only gave him a short smile and waited for space on the path.

When they were out of earshot, he said to Kean, "Never tell anyone your business 'less you have to. Most times when you give out information, you're losing something and gaining nothing in return."

"Yeah . . ." Kean was thinking. "Hawkerman?"

"Yes?"

"All those years ago . . . why did you bring me into the team?"

Hawkerman glanced at him, not surprised, not unfriendly.

"I didn't bring you into the team. Cara did."

He said no more, and kept to the principle of being economical with information when they came to the guard huts around the main well and Dagman's residence, low down where the lake had been deepest. To Kean, the building was like a mansion, and the variously shaped metal props that supported it, put in over the years, made it all the more impressive. Five Cruiser guards sat in shade under the bowed veranda. Two of them were braiding their long hair, which was worn in a tight bun under their steel caps, both as padding and as insulation against the sun's heat. When Hawkerman and Kean were close, two of the Cruisers got to their feet.

"Frumitch," Hawkerman said.

"And who are you?" the younger of the Cruisers asked.

"He's called Hawkerman," the other told him. "Go get Frumitch."

The young Cruiser bent and ducked through the low cat-hide door, and they all waited without words. Eventually a truly repulsive figure came out with the Cruiser. It was not just that he was squat and covered in some form of naturally recurring blisters, for physical defects were not remarkable here: it was the evil that lived in his eyes like a slow-moving worm.

"Hawkerman," he said in a light voice that had a trace of a lisp. A fragment of metal shone in his mouth: a cosmetic implant in an incisor.

"Frumitch. It's been some time."

"So you want something."

"I want some words with Dagman." Hawkerman reached into his bag and brought out a knife, a simple kind used by the poorer people and also as a cheap article for purposes of trading.

"I got a million of them," Frumitch said without expression.

"And you'd like a million more."

"Well, there is that."

Frumitch took the bribe and led the way through a dark anteroom into a series of passages. Kean saw steps leading up to the warehouse above this floor, and then they came to another, even darker room. It was the one that housed Dagman. Frumitch pulled back the hanging over the door.

"Hawkerman. I told him it wasn't a good time, but he was insistent."

A voice came out of the darkness. "Is it day or night?" It was a deep voice, thick and somehow soiled, Kean thought.

"It's day, Dagman," Frumitch lisped back.

"Better be good, then. I'm ready to sleep."

Tinder flared and a taper was lit and applied to a lamp. The room must have been in the middle of the shack for there was no window and precious little air in here. It took

Dagman some seconds to get the lamp lit, and as he did, Kean studied him in the fragile, wavering light from the taper. The top Cruiser had affixed no metal to the voluminous leather shift he wore, and he was naked underneath. Flesh hung down from his upper arms like sleeves full of fat, and his greasy hair tumbled down unbraided so that he resembled an enormous and extremely dangerous old woman. He was around fifty years old, with a heavy, crumpled face that crushed down onto a wide undershot jaw like a bulldog's, with one wayward brown tooth sticking upward out of it. They said he liked his charjaw meat to rot a little before he ate it, so it was softer. You could smell his breath from here. The lamp at last took light, and he leaned back again, half falling onto the pile of skins that was his bed. More skins lined both floor and walls. It was like being in a savage creature's den. The lamp lit only a small area of the room.

"Come where I can see you."

Hawkerman and Kean stepped forward.

"Who's the boy?" Dagman sounded tired and uninterested.

"One of my team."

"He's very white."

"Yes."

"Why's he here?"

"He's my witness. You've got yours." Hawkerman jerked a thumb at Frumitch, behind them.

"He's got someone else here, too," Kean blurted out. His sharp eyes had picked out movement in the far corner of the room; it had seemed like one of the hangings on the wall had eased itself across into the darkest spot of all.

"How do you get eyes that good?" Dagman asked.

For a moment Kean thought it might be Snakebite lurking there, having somehow beaten them to his master. Then the figure detached itself from the shadows and stepped forward. It was a big man, broader than Snakebite, and strangely stooped. He was hidden under a buckskin cloak and a hood that reached so far forward that for all you could see into its depths, there might have been no face within it at all.

"You got anyone else here?" Hawkerman asked with a trace of sarcasm. He was apparently not surprised that Dagman had a bodyguard or assassin near his side.

"No, since you ask. He won't bother us. What's the deal, Hawkerman?"

"It's a problem."

"What problem?"

Hawkerman told, carefully and concisely, the events that had transpired between him and Snakebite. When he was done, Dagman closed his heavy eyelids and ruminated. After a second or two, he said, "You still haven't told me why you're here."

"Snakebite will come along with his account of the story. I want your guarantee that if he makes it a vendetta, you won't back him—and I want him to know it."

"Why wouldn't I back him? Facing down a Cruiser, making use of his transport—that could give men the wrong kind of message. I can't guarantee you anything that would hurt business, you know that."

Then we're all going to die, Kean thought. It didn't seem possible it was going to end like this. They should have stayed in the outlands and never returned.

Hawkerman's tone was as flat as before. "What's bad for business is Cruisers messing with what they don't understand." He got down on his haunches to look Dagman full in the eye. "Out there are all the goods you haven't already got. Out there, we have to look after the things that look after us, or we can't make it back with the goods. It's just that simple. You don't trade water in the flatlands. It's the one thing you offer. You don't tear down whole trees and burn them. He didn't know the rules, so he paid." He got up again and waited.

Dagman considered the angles. His eyes came up and fixed on Kean. "What's your opinion on this?"

Kean looked at Hawkerman, whose gaze did not deviate from Dagman. *He trusts me,* Kean realized.

"Well," he said, and thought of a saying of Hawkerman's: *Don't waste lies where they're not necessary.* He said again, slowly, "Well . . . the country out there, it's hostile, and it's big. I mean *really* big. When you travel, you know how big it is."

Dagman waited, but Kean left it at that. He had almost forgotten about the hooded man when there came a short bark of laughter from him. Dagman turned his heavy head to the man and then back to Kean, and he was smiling, too, showing his few teeth. "You're saying we should know our limitations—stick to running the Lakes?"

"Um . . . well . . . maybe I am."

"Maybe you're right, too."

Hawkerman said, "I wanted you to have this." He took from his bag Snakebite's belt. "It's the tax your man paid, for getting things wrong. Now we're here at the Lakes and asking for a ruling from you, so we pay our taxes to you. Like always. You see, nothing has changed. I have respect."

"*Respect?* You certainly got nerve," Dagman said, and began to shake with laughter. Kean had not known how tense Hawkerman was until he felt the team leader relax at his side. Dagman stopped laughing. "You steal the thing he values most and you give it to me. That's very appealing."

"Well, seemed to me, if you haven't got a use for it, Snakebite could pay you plenty to get it back."

"Oh yes!" The chieftain laughed again. "He will want it back!"

"You tell him he's on his own in all this." Hawkerman tossed the belt to Dagman.

"I will do that," Dagman said, admiring the belt in his hands. "But if there's killing and you start it, we do not have a deal."

"I understand you," Hawkerman said coolly. He nodded to Dagman, and they left the room with Frumitch. There was no doubt in Kean's mind that in that room, men had died in violent circumstances, and he was glad to be out of it.

SEVEN

When they were safely away from the dwelling, Kean said, "Snakebite has a lot of men. Shouldn't you have finished him off when you took his belt?"

"You ever going to learn anything? There's no percentage in putting yourself in the wrong. You listen to me: Snakebite can't just come on in while we're here and cut us up. Not at the Lakes. They belong to Dagman when all's said and done, and he's going to tell Snakebite to hold back, because if Cruisers go around the Lakes killing for personal reasons, it damages confidence in them. Scares people off. See, Kean, once you start to do business, there are little rules that come into being everywhere."

"Yes. I guess so."

"Now, first thing Snakebite's going to do is go right to Dagman and say, 'Look how bad I was treated,' and when he's done that, he's finished because Dagman's greedy and took the belt. To keep it or barter it back, he has to believe he has a right to it in the first place—so that means he has to go along with my side of the story."

"If it had been me, I'd never have brought us back here."

"I don't give up my way of life for scum like Snakebite." Hawkerman tapped him lightly on the back. "You did well in there. Knew where to start and where to stop."

Kean was pleased.

∽

If you were this good at skin maintenance, it was quite easy to save a little filler during lessons. Essa needed less than anyone else, and the extra she secreted in a spare container she strapped under her tunic. Getting hold of maps and duty rosters was harder, and eventually she realized she had to learn them by heart at the workshop and from the copies Bonix was allowed to keep at home. He was delighted at her diligence in learning her trade, so there was no need to be secretive there. Getting herself put down for duty during a Feast Day was the easiest thing of all, since every Arconian wanted to be present at the games in the Measureless Chamber, and those that couldn't fit in there created their own sports events in other arenas.

She had discovered a ten-minute opportunity on the third level, when the corridors around the Archive should be empty. Twenty minutes later, there came another ten minutes without passing patrols. There would still be a guard on the doors, but she had no need of doors. Not now.

It was corner work. Only the fear factor gave her doubt in her ability to cut a right-angle flap close to the floor at the junction where the Archive met with the Conference Chamber. Right around the next corner were more guards on the door of the Conference Chamber. None of the Pacifiers would leave their posts—not for anything, she kept telling herself. She was going to learn all she could about Arcone, and if it took more than one of these forays to do it, well, so be it. The days of blind duty were done.

Everything went smoothly. Walking the corridors, timing her moves up the ramps to the third level—getting into place, at least, was easy. But she felt so exposed under the permanent phosphor lights. She was about to become a criminal. She walked past the doors to the Archive, carrying her notes tablet as a talisman to ward off questioning. Head held high, she went past the two guards and turned into the last corridor. Ahead of her was the corner, getting nearer and nearer: her destination and her destiny.

Now she could see nothing else. She couldn't even hear well with the blood that was pounding in her head. The corner had not been rebonded for a long time, she realized, so her task would be easier than it might have been. She knelt down and took out her scalpel. Hesitated. This was it.

"Elessa, of Bonix and Marran."

The quiet and terrible statement came, it seemed, almost at her shoulder. She jumped to her feet, the speed of her movement betraying her guilt, she was sure, and turned to the voice, already knowing who it was.

Grollat.

He had no particular expression on his face, and there were no clues in his dark, deep voice, either.

"What are you doing, Elessa?"

"I—I saw an imperfection. I wanted a closer look."

"It's not usual for a scout to make examinations while holding a scalpel. And if I had not arrived at the moment that I did, what would you have done with the scalpel?"

She blundered on desperately. "I thought I might see whether there was plastic fatigue—farther in."

He said dryly, "How much farther in?"

She had the sense not to say anything now. Silence, the refuge of the frightened criminal.

Grollat held out his hand for the scalpel. "Give it to me."

She did so, wordlessly.

He contemplated the razor-sharp implement, turning it this way and that in his hand. "I could make you tell more lies. There's a skill to it—leading the victim on. Or I could have waited until you cut the wall. Until you could see into the Archive itself. Then what would your punishment have been?"

"I don't know."

"I do." He eyed her dispassionately. "But I didn't do those things. Come with me."

"Where?" Oh no—why did she always speak before thinking?

He was walking away. Should she run? Where? There was nowhere she could hide and no one who would hide her. He knew it and did not look back. She hurried to catch up with him and walked by his side.

They passed the Pacifiers at the Archive doors and walked the winding corridors until they reached the ramp that curved down to the next level. Along a hallway, down another level, passing the stupendous walls of the Measureless Chamber. From it the shouts and calls of the hundreds of spectators rang out through the empty walkways they negotiated at the main junction. The sound was so animated that Essa could almost picture the colorful scene in the arena, with families leaping up from their seats on the stands to urge on their favorites in some race or game. She could have been in there right now, celebrating, carefree, only a very small part in the scheme of things but a person who belonged. Instead, she was going with this fearsome man to—what? And where?

Grollat stopped at a lift portal. Once the few lifts had been powered; now they were operated by a pulley system. Two of his men stood guard at the opening. Grollat nodded to them, and one of them called down the shaft, "Gather up!"

Essa waited with Grollat until the tall rectangular box rose up into place. It was propelled by a Pacifier who hauled at one of the two synthetic chains at the side of the lift. When it came to a stop, perfectly aligned in the portal, Grollat took Essa by the arm and they stepped in.

"Pull below," Grollat ordered, and the attendant took the other chain, bent down, and pulled. They began to descend the dimly lit shaft. But where were they *going*? She opened her mouth to speak, and at the same instant, Grollat shook his head at her and turned his eyes to the Pacifier. She shut her mouth.

They passed another portal, and Essa saw a reservoir engineer going by in the corridor, recognizable by the waterproof tunic he wore. So—that was it. They were going down to the reservoir, and she would be incarcerated in one of the cells . . .

However, when they stopped and left the lift, they were in a wide hallway facing a single door. There were no guards here. This was one of the few doors that had a lock, and Grollat took out a key. On one side the hallway opened into a corridor; the other side was blocked by one of the cumbersome pillars that rose through the center of Arcone on the lower levels.

Grollat pushed the door open and walked in. Essa followed.

They were in the main room of a three-chamber apartment. It was brightly lit by a whole series of phosphor globes in the ceiling, which seemed strange here, since there was some kind of window, a long thin one in the far wall, which let in yet more light. Had the apartment belonged to Essa, she would have left it as dim as possible; as it was, you saw all too clearly how messy the place was. Clothes were scattered on the couch along with an unfinished plate of food. The walls were devoid of decoration, and there was a layer of dust on the floor.

"This is . . . ?" Essa ventured, although she had guessed the answer already.

"This is where you live if you are Commander of the Pacifiers. It's cool and it's spacious and it has a view."

Grollat went to the window in the far wall and slid open one of its three sections, allowing damp air to rush in. Essa joined him. The view was of the reservoir, from the highest point in the cavern. This window was a narrow slit cut through the rock . . . she could see the cells opposite her and the path that led up to them, and the metal cage hanging from the smooth ceiling, high above everything except this one window.

The cage was what Grollat was looking at.

He said flatly, "You're nearly full grown. For what you did today, you would sit in that cage for some days, and then, when a suitable audience was gathered, my men would lower you into the water. They would lower you many feet below the surface. The assembled dignitaries would not see you drown, of course. They would merely sit and wait for some thirty minutes until the cage was raised. It is a great honor to die in this fashion, in the precious substance. The water is purifying and would cleanse you of your crime."

"Yes, I see . . . ," Essa said faintly.

"If you look hard, you'll see the block-and-tackle system. Clever. The cage can go straight down, or it can be drawn in toward the Self-Examination Cells—if you were wondering how anyone gets into it."

"I wasn't."

Grollat's voice stayed low and level. "Your mother and father were placed in that cage, not long after you were born.

They would have hung there in, well, suspense, shall we say, until the day the cage descended into the water and stayed deep beneath the surface for thirty minutes."

"What are you talking about?"

"At that time I was not senior enough to be admitted to the spectacle. There were two others in the cage as well. Since then I have witnessed the cleansing of several wrong-doers. It can be a noisy business if they start to scream. I've often thought the entire population should be allowed to watch these occasions. It would have an effect that might make my job easier."

"I'm sorry, I don't understand you. What do you mean about my mother and father?"

"They died. Bonix and Marran are not your parents."

In her mind Essa said, *It's just a lie. He wants to hurt me. Why?* She said aloud, "It's not true."

He was looking at her, reading her pain, smiling slightly. Their eyes met. And she knew. Just knew. *It is true. Why else would he say it?*

A sick-making feeling of love and guilt and loss swept over her. Oh no. She loved Bonix and Marran, but she hadn't been loving enough, and now they were taken from her. She swallowed and controlled her breathing and managed to say, "So who were they? My real mother and father? What had they done?"

He evidently approved of the effort she had made. "You're very calm about it. Your father was a brilliant manufacturer of paints, and your mother was a musician.

You need know no more than that. They were a much-envied couple and loved by their friends."

"Were they your friends?"

"No. I hardly knew them. You might say their crime was to care too much. They were clever people and impatient with the ways of Arcone. They questioned the order of things. They spoke to many, telling them that it was unjust that knowledge should be kept from the common people. They organized secret meetings and discussed the forcing through of new laws, to make information available to all. They were betrayed to my predecessor and were cleansed. You—innocent of any crime against the city—were placed with a childless couple. Bonix and Marran."

The foundations of her life were exploded. It had taken only seconds. Her true parents had been criminals. No—good people, with good intentions. Now she herself was a wrongdoer, and with what fate in store?

"All right, Commander. I believe you. Now what am I doing here?"

The bold words did not disguise her fear, and Grollat smiled. "You think that I want something of you?"

"I just don't know why I'm here."

She glanced around the room, noticing again the disorder. He read her expression of distaste and said, "I have a wife, Essa, but she is not well. She spends most of her time in the infirmary, where they try to persuade her that it is not good for her to consume mind-altering substances.

She seeks tranquility through chemical means. We, too, have known difficult times."

Later she regretted not taking him up on that last piece of information. She might have learned more about what motivated him. For now all she said was, "I don't like being here with you, Commander."

He took her by the arm, turning her so that she had to face him, squeezing into her flesh, his voice becoming harsh. "You're not meant to like it! And I have no interest in whether you like me, either. I'm not likeable—I don't expect people to like me." He added savagely, "I wouldn't be very good at my job if people *liked* me—would I?"

"No," she said quietly, not wanting to enrage him further.

"I brought you hear to look and listen. Your parents were not obedient Arconians and neither are you. Maybe it's inherited. There are people I keep my eye on, and you are one of them. I have watched you and told my men to watch you—roaming where you have no right. But I have no interest in punishing the young. If I don't have to, I won't. I choose not to punish you."

"Not at all?"

He let go of her. "All I want of you is that you learn your lesson. *It is not possible to defy Arcone.*" He stared at her, willing the thought deep into her mind, and then went back to the window overlooking the reservoir and closed the panel. The damp draught was shut out. He turned back to her. "You must understand that I have put myself in a difficult situation here. I should not have told you what I have. Please remember: if you confront your foster parents with your knowledge, it can only lead to trouble for all of us. Perhaps especially for them. Do you understand?"

"Yes. I shouldn't speak of it."

"And you won't speak of it?"

It was so hard. How could she not? She still loved them—couldn't help it. And that was what settled the matter, in a defining instant. She must not do anything that could damage them. *Ever*.

"I won't speak of it."

"Good. I will have to tell Bonix that you have been seen straying from your work duties on occasion. You will receive a single demerit. It should not be a hindrance to your future, if you wish to rise in society."

Essa was confused and relieved at the same time. "Should I thank you?"

He shrugged. "It won't make any difference to anything."

She had to anyway, even if she did not understand his motives in this. "Thank you, Commander."

She meant it, and he must have heard the sincerity in her voice. All he said was, "All right—you've said it. Now let's go."

As they went out of the apartment, Grollat commented, "I'm not here much. Too busy. Needs cleaning, I know."

The remark was so commonplace, it was as though the strange interview had been officially closed and now they were back in normalcy, where there was no opportunity to ask more about herself, or her parents, or the difficulty the Commander had known in his own life.

He led her in silence by the walkways, back up through the levels, past the festivities in the Measureless Chamber, bringing her at last to her own apartment.

"Wait in there. Your parents will come to you when the games are over."

For a moment, she felt he hesitated, and she could have reopened their conversation, or at least thanked him again, but then he turned away from her: a dangerous, lonely man whom she did not understand.

She herself was lonelier than she had ever been.

EIGHT

With regular intake of sweet petal concentrate, Wailing Joe made good progress back to health, and although he was still very underweight, Hawkerman did not attempt to dissuade him when he announced he was ready to become an active team member again. There was a lot that needed to be done: the polishing up and selling of some of the goods, and a careful overhaul of the tent.

They had seen Snakebite once after his team limped into the Lakes. The Cruiser had gone straight to see Dagman, and it seemed he had got the message, for he had simply ignored Hawkerman's team when he walked past their tent with a couple of his followers. He was wearing the belt. Hawkerman said, "He'll have his ideas—be sure of that. I don't want any one going near him."

Hawkerman was fretful. His brother had not yet returned. The team went out to make inquiries and pooled their knowledge before an evening meal, talking quietly as they sat under the big tree in the dying light from the sun.

Kean had been paired with one of the mute twins, Wil, who nodded affirmation as he made his report.

"I asked around the blacksmiths. Fireface placed an order for some small fast trailers. The blacksmiths haven't delivered because they haven't been paid. There's a rumor he's dead, but no one knows who started it. And if he's got a big team here, all I can say is they're keeping themselves very quiet."

Wailing Joe agreed. "There's not one person who'll admit they held allegiance to him."

Barb chipped in. "He was supposed to come back two weeks ago—that's what I hear. You ask me, when he didn't, it just all kind of evaporated. They're disbanded."

Hawkerman said, "I think it's worse than that."

"How so?" Cara asked.

"There's Cancher—weapons expert. Cancher was a supporter from way back. Now he says he was only working for goods, like some of the others. He's lying. So my guess is someone's been leaning on them hard. Breaking them up."

"Dagman?" Ax queried.

"Someone who can put fear in you. Dagman, Frumitch . . . any one of the Cruiser teams."

Kean said thoughtfully, "I guess if Fireface did attack the Pyramid and it went wrong, the Bleachers would retaliate. Hit the Lakes."

"You got it, Kean," Hawkerman concurred, "Most here don't want to shake things up—they got it good enough and that's how they want to keep it."

"So we'll never know."

"I don't care about my brother's crazy notions. I do care about him. I need to know if he's alive."

Wailing Joe observed, "The Season's well late. There's still not much sign of it coming yet awhile. He could make it back even now."

"And if he doesn't? Then I wouldn't know anything about him till the Season's over. And if he was dead when the storms hit, he could be buried under the topsoil somewhere, and then I'd never know what happened."

Cara looked anxious. "We can't go back out now. It's too late."

"And if we did," Barb said, "you can bet Snakebite would come right after us."

Hawkerman got up. "Sorry to disturb you, but come night we're moving out."

"What," Kean said, "into the flatlands?"

The rest of the team had been shocked into silence. Hawkerman said, "Not the flatlands. The Rocks. If Snakebite follows, we can dig in there. We're going to see Skyfly."

The only man in the valley with any form of aerial transport. The human vulture, who used that transport to search for the dead and take their belongings before anyone else came upon them.

⌒

Essa had waited a long time for Bonix and Marran to return to the apartment. Apprehension had consumed her less than the awful depression she felt.

They are not my parents, she had thought over and over, and it hurt every time. She would welcome their anger about her misdemeanors, as reported to them, because nothing—*nothing*—would change her deep affection for them. They had taken her in and done their best by her. With a twinge of shame, she allowed herself to wonder if Marran would have been more demonstrative with a child of her own flesh. Bonix's deep affection was far more obvious; he liked to see Essa as an extension of himself, and *his* reaction was the one she dreaded.

With good cause. When it had come, it had been a father's reaction, no doubt about it. You would have thought she had murdered the entire Council in their beds. Within moments of his arrival in the apartment, she had not been able to stop feelings of resentment vaulting to the fore as the scene played out, feelings so strong they made her disregard how far she had been in the wrong. How could he reprimand her like this if all she had done was walk around a little where she wasn't supposed to?

Bonix's dignity had been hit hard, and he found a great many words with which to express the thought that she had let him down badly.

"Ungrateful . . . unruly . . . untrustworthy . . .

"Shameful . . . irresponsible . . . unworthy . . .

"Reckless disregard . . . willful disobedience . . .

"I don't recognize you as my child!"

Essa had become so angry she wanted to shout, *I'm not, though, am I?*

He had not given her time, charging onward in a choked voice. "The Commander was generous in the extreme. I put it down to his respect for me and your mother. A single demerit? Well, I'll tell you, my girl—"

I'm not your girl.

"—I'll tell you, it's not enough. In my capacity as your superior, I am going to recommend a period of Low Toil. Then we'll see if you still want to go your willful way!"

"That's not fair! You don't get Low Toil unless you've been given at least a double demerit!"

"Which you should have been!"

"But I wasn't!"

"I have to say," Marran had interjected anxiously, "there seems no need to make it so plain to everyone that Elessa has misbehaved. Surely the Commander was thinking of just that when he acted so compassionately."

"It's not a question of what the Commander thinks. It's a question of what *I* believe to be right and wrong. I want it clearly seen that I do not countenance antisocial behavior, even from my own family—*especially* from my own family."

"Well, thank you!" Essa had said, tight-lipped. "Now we know all you're interested in is how it makes *you* look."

"Go to your room!"

She went. So in the end, it had been a real family argument. How weird.

And here she was now, lying waiting in her darkened room. Waiting because she knew her mother would come to her.

And of course Marran came, to be understanding, to soothe. She told Essa not to be too upset about Bonix and said, "He loves you—he worries for you."

"He worries for himself."

"It's hard being a parent sometimes. He's only trying to do the right thing. For you, as well as the city. You must believe that."

Essa turned to face the wall.

"The work won't be too hard," her mother reassured her. "It will soon all be forgotten. We will be as we were."

No. Never again.

Marran listened to the stubborn silence for a minute or two and then left the room.

Essa turned onto her back and looked up to where the ceiling would be if she could see it. What a day. That defining moment in Grollat's quarters . . . everything had altered in a fraction of a second. This horrible fight she'd had with her parents who were not her parents . . .

And there was no one in the world she could talk to about any of it.

She did not belong here in the pyramid city of Arcone. She was an outsider whose parents had been killed by an unjust society. What she could do about that plain fact, she did not know, but in order to be in a position to do anything, she was going to have to go further with her duplicity.

Yes. Pretend more than ever that she was a good little Arconian. Take tips from poor Veramus, always so anxious to please. Show no dissent, take no more chances, do nothing; be ready.

For what?

Be ready.

Under the pain of her circumstances, a pulse of excitement began to beat.

∽

An hour before dawn, they slipped out from the Lakes. The darkness was no guarantee they would not be seen, for unless his character had undergone a complete change, Snakebite would have spies noting their every movement. Hawkerman wanted to make the bulk of the journey in daylight in order to be able to watch behind them.

Making their getaway, they traveled at a heavy trot for as long as possible, slogging on in the growing heat underneath the wispy cirrus clouds that floated above, as insubstantial as breath. Here, where the valley narrowed at its end, the rocky hills that enclosed it were only two days' journey away, and with that in mind, they had determined to travel almost continuously. It would be harder for Snakebite to mount an attack up in the Rocks.

The destitute made this journey, those who had lost the trading game and had nothing. The Rocks offered meat, in the form of porcupines and burrowing animals, and shelter in caves. They also offered dangers aplenty: landslides; every known reptile; and the caves were home to the big cats, dusty-gray and ferocious, attacking anything that moved. Many of them were enraged with pain, their pitted skins scarred by battle and by the rock splinters that exploded like shrapnel at night, when the bitter cold contracted stone which had warmed and expanded during the day.

By the time the broken boulders were well in sight, every member of the team was leg-weary and gasping. Wailing Joe had no hauling duties; for the others, the trailer weighed more with each step. Kean felt the pace less than anyone else, and Hawkerman urged him to go on ahead.

"Get in among the rocks. Use your eyes. I want a site we can defend."

It was quiet. His feet slipped loudly on the shifting shale and pebbles. The pebbles became rocks, and the rocks became bigger and steeper. He clambered upward and arrived at an outcrop halfway up the valley walls. The ground fell away here into a deep hollow. He slithered down into it until he was standing on what might make a decent campsite. By standing on tiptoe, he could look down at the team below. Kean gauged that if they dismantled the trailer, they could get the gear up this far, where no one could travel fast or silently. They would be just about hidden, and there would be no chance of a surprise attack.

Unless there was someone already up here, lying in wait . . .

In the corner of his eye, Kean saw a flapping mass descending on him from above. He reacted, rolling onto his back and raising his legs, squeezing them back against his chest in a human spring. The flapping mass was a man whose cloak flew behind him and whose body thumped down onto the soles of Kean's feet. Kean leaned back onto his shoulder blades and kicked his legs with vicious speed, throwing the human bundle far over his head. The man was as light as a hollow-boned bird and flew far, smack into the edge of the outcrop. When Kean had twisted around and bounced to his feet, he saw the man struggling back up, trying to reach the knife he had dropped. Kean got there first and kicked it away. He drew his own knife with one hand and grabbed the man's hair with the other.

"You be still."

The man's eyes rolled in his head as he felt the blade against his throat. "Yes. I will," he whispered.

"We'll stay as we are awhile."

"Oh yes."

A minute or two later, Hawkerman hauled himself up onto the stone.

"Saw you had some action. Who you got there?"

"I think he was going to kill me."

"Rob you, that's for sure."

He walked over to look at Kean's prisoner.

"One of Skyfly's boys. He rides the basket." He took the man's face in his hand, squeezing it. The man was hollow-cheeked enough already, with milky eyes. "You're not going to do anything, now are you?"

"Oh no," the man whispered. "No, no." As he gazed upward at Hawkerman, Kean saw that he was totally sunblind.

"You watch him, Kean," Hawkerman said, and let the man go, surveying the rocky hollow. "Good site. Do us well."

Within a couple of hours, the tent was in place on the outcropping, and the twins were guarding it while the rest of the team made their way up higher over the boulders, going to the gas geysers where Skyfly made his home. The sunblind man led the way, surefooted in his own territory when daylight failed. They saw none of the big cats, only heard one coughing nearby. At this time of day, the cats were exactly the same color as the rocks.

They saw the balls of flaming gas leaping into the sky long before they descended the other side of the rocky hills and came to a low plateau on the margins of the Gray, a desolate place where gases erupted between fissures in the rock.

The team walked in under the eyes of all. Skyfly's hangers-on made their homes in caves down here, dependent on the master of the skies for handouts and protection. In return, they serviced the balloon, which was a full-time job. In the interests of weight, it was made of the lightest snake skins that could be found. Reptile hunting—often with fatal consequences for the hunter—was a year-round activity here, as was water fetching. The nearest natural well was a day away, and the water tasted of sulfur when it arrived.

Lying loosely folded, weighed down with stones all around, the big balloon was like a gargantuan snake curled up. The balls of flame were caused by Skyfly burning off excess fuel from the ground, an operation so dangerous that only he would do it. Like a priest in the service of the monstrous expanse of snakeskin that was his livelihood, he himself wore reptile skins, a tiny bent figure of a man whose iron-gray hair was so unruly that he might have been charged with static. His back was to them, and the team watched as he set his flaming torch at a spot in the air about a yard above ground level, and as if he were a magician, another fireball of gas ascended into the sky. Beyond him the broken terrain of the Gray was dark, and the impassable mountains were black in the distance.

"You're going to catch light yourself one of these days," Hawkerman observed.

The balloonist turned. Took note of the strangers.

"You have to do it when you're not tapping gas for flying," he answered casually. "It builds up just underneath the surface, and then you can get explosions. When it's close to the Season, you might have a little lightning in the wrong place and—whoosh—we all fly!" The old man grinned toothlessly at his own joke. "What you doing with Spitless?"

"That his name?" Hawkerman said, interested. "He tried to murder one of my men."

"All by himself? He doesn't learn, do you, Spitless?"

The man they had captured shambled over to Skyfly. "No," he whispered, conciliatory.

Skyfly ignored him. He was still looking at Hawkerman, and his voice became thin and hard. "What do you want?"

"I want a trip in the sky. I'm looking for something."

"It's too late. I've quit for the Season."

"There'd be time, the way things are looking."

Skyfly looked him up and down. "You're too heavy, anyway."

"Sure, if you say so. But I've got someone here who owes me and who's light enough and sees real good. He'd go up for me." Hawkerman turned to Kean.

Who did not appreciate the idea one bit. "What do you mean, I owe you?"

"Saved you from some charjaws not long back. You can't have forgotten that. I think I should be allowed to choose how you pay."

NINE

Essa hated Arcone. Hated the order in everything and hated the orders she was given. She hated being told to find beauty in her surroundings, hated being told she was lucky to be here. Hated always being told exactly where to go and what to do.

The period of punishment hadn't been too bad for the first days, when she was spraying chemical growth-enhancers on the tight little buds in the indoor fields where plastic grew. Here dwarf oilseed plants were injected with the genes that produced plastic polymers in them. It was not healthy work, the spraying, and the workers in the fields were always glad of the help provided by punishment duties.

The advantage of the plastic grown in the Pyramid was at the same time its disadvantage: it was biodegradable to one degree or another, depending on the gene material used and the conditions of growth. The longer-lasting plastics took proportionately longer to grow.

Eventually all plastic artifacts lost their elasticity and were disassembled and turned into a kind of plastic compost useful for the manufacture of non-fade paints. It was this composting work she had gone onto when the spraying was finished. Sorting types of material, hastening the rotting process by warming and endless mashing, straining the resulting goo until it was free from impurities—all amid a smell worse than Maxamar's body odors. She hated it.

At home Bonix maintained a chilly aloofness in their relations. While Marran was being kind enough, she also had a slightly cool quality about her—but then, she always had.

When the day came, what a release it would be when Essa could *talk* to someone about who she really was.

∽

Skyfly had said it was too risky at this time of year. Furthermore, it took three days to fill the balloon with gas. And when they got up there, he would be flying with a novice and not his usual crew member—the dim-witted Spitless. Since these arguments were put forward during a journey to the team's tent to view what they had to offer, Hawkerman knew it was a matter of price.

"My brother had two whole teams with him," he told Skyfly. "That's a lot of weapons and some fine goods. Plenty of personal belongings, good clothing. I'll pay you, anyway, and if you find any or all of them and they're dead, well, you'll get the goods on top."

"He had that cloak, didn't he, Fireface? I always did admire that," Skyfly ruminated. "Lightweight but durable. My kind of thing."

"Most handsome, yes."

Although he knew Hawkerman well, Kean was taken aback at his lack of emotion when discussing how the balloon pilot might be able to plunder prize possessions from his dead brother's body. You could just see the twisted little man salivating over the rich pickings that might be his. Nevertheless, Skyfly did not allow this attractive dream to destroy his common sense.

"Most likely he's alive," he said sourly. "What's to say he didn't just decide to wait out the Season someplace else?"

Hawkerman said, "He had something he wanted to do. It had a time limit on it, and he was hurrying for the Lakes when we met up with him. I can give you the course he would have taken. It's not like you've got to traverse the entire valley. In any case, you'll do it when you see what we got." He kept up the note of confidence. "The usual conditions will apply—half now, half on completion."

The outcome of the trading session was inevitable. Skyfly's bargaining position was unassailable: he had something Hawkerman wanted, so he could charge his own price. After several hours, he had evaluated all their trading goods and earmarked the best of them for himself. It was the only time Kean had ever seen Hawkerman come out of a deal badly.

The team leader allowed his rancor to show through after shaking hands on the deal. He jerked his thumb at

Kean and said to Skyfly, "You don't do this search good and my man here will kill you." He looked over at Kean. "You could do that, couldn't you?"

Kean stared at the flier, weighing him up and letting him know it, intimidating him in the way you could if you had studied how Hawkerman did these things. He waited, and Skyfly twitched a little under his steady gaze.

"Yes," Kean said. "I can do that."

Saying it, he knew he meant it, and for a moment, he did not like himself. But it was useless to threaten unless you were prepared to act on it. Maybe it was all right if you were only doing what you had to in order to survive. If you only did what you had to do, maybe that kept you halfway decent, halfway honorable.

Still, it was hard to be a Wanderer. Potentially damaging to something precious you were born with.

❧

Gas was channeled into the snakeskin envelope at an almost imperceptible rate, traveling through well-greased tubes made of animal intestines. Waiting for take-off made Kean jumpy. The rest of the team had gone back to their tent site on the other side of the valley wall. Hawkerman did not like the idea of having his forces split. He would not be shaken from his conviction that Snakebite had set someone to track them.

Kean had a cave to himself, and if he looked out during the cold, starlit nights, he could see the reptilian balloon growing, a lazily shifting, living creature. He looked often and slept little. Ax had lent him a thick cloak to act as a blanket; it smelled of the trailer and made Kean wish he was with the others, instead of being here among enemies. The desiccated halfwit, Spitless, was deeply affronted that he had lost his place in the basket beside Skyfly, and Kean felt his brooding eyes on him the whole time. He was fairly sure that, if he could, Spitless would slide a knife between his ribs, so he arranged tripwires and scattered pebbles all around the cave mouth. During the second night he was woken from an exhausted doze by the *click* of stones disturbed. He reached for his knife as a frail figure scuttled away. Somewhere not far away, a boulder discharged a frozen shard of rock with a sound like a rifle shot. Kean drew the borrowed cloak around himself and shivered.

However slowly it moves, time gets there in the end. At last, on the third morning, the balloon was almost fully inflated. Kean stood near it to watch the final preparations. Most of Skyfly's followers were a little in awe of the Wanderer who had come among them; as they rushed around the balloon with lines to tie it down, or brought stones for ballast, they glanced at him with smiles of respect.

"You wouldn't get any of that lot into the sky," Skyfly observed, coming to his side. "They ain't crazy enough. That's why I got Spitless. But you do as I tell you and we might make it."

Working as a true team, the shabby outcasts had rapidly assembled two aluminum gantries, from the top of which they worked on the balloon once it was pulling moodily at the lines holding it down. First they fitted an arrangement of short wings and airfoils, which gave the appearance of being a kind of utility belt on the now spherical serpent. The aids to navigation were fashioned from strong lizard skin and vulture feathers, and were braced by bone like a real bird's wing. The lines that worked each individual device were fastened to the basket when finally it was hoisted into place. It was little more than a flat-bottomed leather bucket, strengthened with plastic struts.

One by one, the stones that were to be the ballast were hoisted into the bucket under the supervision of Skyfly, who selected each one himself, making sure there was a wide variety of weights available to him.

He put on his mottled flying hat, the one article of clothing not made from reptile skin. It had a long visor on it that would shield his eyes from the sun.

"You're not taking any headgear?" he asked Kean.

Kean shook his head. "I don't burn."

"You might where we're going. You want real heat, go high like we're going to."

"What's the hat made from?"

Skyfly looked around furtively. "Porcupine skin. But I tell them it came from a man. Keeps 'em in good order. You hop in now."

The lines holding down the balloon remained taut. A dozen men stood around as Kean and Skyfly got up into the basket. Kean tripped almost at once. There were a number of cat skins strewn around haphazardly, as well as all the ballast stones. This was not a luxury mode of transport, and the basket felt worryingly insubstantial. You could feel its floor bulging under your feet when you moved around.

All about them lines were being loosed alternately—untie one, leave one holding—and now Kean felt the balloon tugging upward, anxious to leave the earth behind.

It had not taken Skyfly long to explain the theory of balloon flight. Go down by releasing gas, go up again by releasing ballast. Now Kean swayed in the basket suddenly, hit by his tiredness after two nights of uneasy sleep. Well, all he had to do was follow orders. He should be able to manage that.

Then Skyfly was grinning and shouting, "Cut me loose!"

The rest of the retaining lines were severed cleanly in one swift motion, and at once the balloon began to rise majestically. It was such a stately ascent, so direct and so glorious in its silent ease, that Kean's fear gave way almost at once to pure exhilaration. As they rose ever higher, directly up into the sky, huge tracts of his world were displayed to him. He clung to the rim of the basket and looked. The broken valley walls they had left already seemed an insignificant feature, diminishing into a long bony spine, and his eye was drawn to the unknown, the craggy lands beyond the valley. First there were the broad gray wastes, and then it really got rough out there. Fearsome. Mountains burst from the disintegrating landscape like an eruption of shattered teeth, split by deep gorges and bottomless ravines. There was no color in the landscape, and no hope of survival out there.

Balanced in the center of the basket, Skyfly was oblivious to him, busy working two thin leather lines attached to ailerons. Moving cautiously, Kean edged by him and peered over the other side.

Here was his own world. In contrast to the Gray, it was a more warm and welcoming color, sort of light brown, mostly.

His eye went to the great Pyramid at the head of the valley. Now he saw how it dominated the scene: it must be even bigger than he had realized. Even from here, he could see how at the top, where it was rounder, the panels were translucent, shining, showing like a bald spot on top of a human head. The windmills all around were a host of tiny dots in close-cropped cornfields of joyous yellow. What a miracle of order and civilization . . .

And how soon it ended. He could see the Big White behind the Pyramid, stretching outward into flat infinity, and looking the other way he could begin to appreciate how vast the valley was. He could just make out the line of rocky cliffs on the far side, but otherwise there was nothing but the outlands, which just got wider and wider, rolling along forever: the plains he had walked since he was a small child.

He dared himself to look straight down. The ground was going sideways—they were beginning to move fast down the Valley now, away from the Pyramid. Something below caught his eye for a split second. He was already turning his head to watch how Skyfly controlled their flight, and so disregarded what he had half seen.

Skyfly was tying off his lines on the edge of the basket. He did not have to raise his voice in order to be heard. "We caught a thermal already. Warm winds you get up here. We're on our way!"

Keen nodded and looked back down to where three specks moved across the plains. From up here, they seemed to move very slowly, traveling from the direction of the Pyramid.

Only they weren't moving so very slowly when you worked it out.

Cruiser wagons. Snakebite. Who else would venture out toward the Rocks at this time of year?

Skyfly had joined him. "What you got there?"

No point in lying about it. "Looks like some wagons."

The old man squinted down. "That's what I make it out to be. You got good eyes, all right. There's not many could see anything that far off. Yeah, not trailers. Cruiser wagons. Looks like trouble."

Feeling the old man's gaze on him, Kean faked suspicion. "What do you know about this? What are they doing out there?"

"I couldn't say. My trading's done long since." Skyfly returned the distrustful look with interest. "Did anyone know you were heading this way?"

"Not that I know of."

"My people are unprotected back there." As if possible carnage among his followers was a cheerful thought, Skyfly grinned, breaking the tension. "Well, life is short, boy—and we're up here—so whatever gives down there, *we* got nothing to worry about."

A second later, the basket keeled over to one side, and they had to hold on to stop themselves spilling out. Skyfly worked his way back to his lines. Hot winds were buffeting at them. "This isn't nothing!" he shouted. "We'll get through this!"

Kean hung onto the rim of the basket, feeling faintly sick, either from the movement of the balloon or the horrible uncertainty that had hit him. Sure. Oh sure. Get through this and whatever else came their way and finally return, with luck, to what? Maybe there would be no Hawkerman left to report to. No team at all.

Skyfly yelled for help, and Kean shuffled over to help him with the lines, obeying the bellowed instructions blindly.

∽

Essa and Veramus were in Tranquility, one of the blue rooms laid out with low seating and tables, a place where you could browse through stultifyingly correct poems and writings about Arcone. Here friends met after work to talk in low voices and sip water in moderation. After the rains had come, the water dispenser would be restored to its place in the corner; at this time of year, you brought your own drink.

"Look," Veramus said proudly. He picked out a sheet of paper from those scattered on their table.

Essa read aloud, "'The Shape of Water.' Oh—it's yours, Veramus."

He smiled modestly. "It is." He read out the poem.

"From rock runs water,
Clear, caressing, wearing down.
My hand passes through it,
No form of its own,
Shaping the stone."

"Yes—good. Very good, Veramus." She caught herself sighing and said firmly, "No, I mean, tremendous. The short ones are the hardest, too. It's really good."

"Well, I'm d-d-doing what I can," he said smugly. "What about y-you?"

"Oh, I'm behaving myself," Essa said dully.

"It's not enough. D-do what I do—m-make yourself seen and heard—p-paint or sing or wr-write some p-p-poems. I'll do one for you, if you like."

"No thanks. I'm all right. It was only a demerit and a little Low Toil."

"Well, it's your life. It won't c-count against you forever," he joked with difficulty. "I'd swap any day!"

She looked away from him, embarrassed by his pain. They had *him*, all right. Since his release from captivity, he spent almost every moment working, trying to make up for his thought crime.

The bland blue walls suggested a banal change of subject. "It's lovely in here, isn't it?"

And about as tedious as you could get, like poor Veramus.

She had gone back to her own work today, and it was so different. The gloss had gone off her chosen career before she'd hardly started. All the time she felt there were eyes watching her now. The Pacifiers. Her foster parents . . .

From birth she had been marked down as a potential troublemaker, and knowing it didn't make her want to conform. The opposite, in fact. And a moment would come. It *would*. Before that time, they couldn't get her again. She was guarding against her natural impetuosity. Thinking before she spoke. Saying nothing spontaneous, not to Veramus, not to anyone.

A moment would come.

TEN

Kean had not envisaged spending the night floating three hundred yards above ground level, where the thermals could not reach them and neither could anything else.

"We'll get some drift, but not a whole lot," Skyfly reassured him, after letting out some gas from the balloon so that they descended beneath the winds.

The cat skins became blankets. They had not been properly cured and gave off a scent of putrefaction. Kean buried himself beneath some of them in a fetal curl. He felt Skyfly's foot touching his ankle and heard the old man cackle, "Cozy, isn't it? We ain't friends, boy, which is why I don't mind knowing exactly where you are."

So it was to be another largely sleepless night, then. Kean put one hand on the handle of his knife and imagined Skyfly doing the same.

He found it odd how tiring it was, just hanging on and watching the world go by. The fatigue was increased by the strain of keeping super-watchful as they searched. He was continually fooled by the movement of wildlife down there. Greenbacks and charjaws, and the larger lizards.

Every now and then he saw richer colors where the water was . . . or had been. The valley's nature was to throw up an oasis and then withdraw it. He looked most carefully in the clusters of trees they flew over, because if Fireface had decided to wait out the Season, he was likely to be found in one of them. Kean looked for movement, for signs of life, for something unusual. He watched for living human beings and feared to find dead ones.

The next morning, breakfast came from a small sack: a few ounces of water and some jellified lizard leg. Kean forced himself to eat while Skyfly tucked in with gusto. They watched each other eating, saying nothing. It would be another very long day. Skyfly's intention was to sweep the valley floor on a line laid down by Hawkerman after the deal was made. The team leader had drawn a rough map of the valley in the dirt and plotted Fireface's most likely route. Now he knew how gigantic their homeland was, Kean realized there was little hope of finding Hawkerman's brother.

At last the flier spat out a bone and stood up in the basket. The gauzy strips of cirrus cloud were almost motionless above. "No sign of storms. And I got a good feeling about this morning."

He chose which ballast stones to throw overboard and the balloon rose up again in search of the thermals.

Before the sun was at its highest, the search was done. The land was dry and featureless, and the two stationary trailers were not hard to spot. They stood in the middle of nowhere, reflecting the sunlight like a distress signal. A sense of foreboding drew Kean's mouth into a tight line.

Skyfly was not so reticent, letting out a whoop of triumph.

"Yahoo! That is the sight I longed for! This is so *fine*!"

He pulled on a line to vent gas from the balloon, and they swooped downward. Once they were below the reach of the thermals, they traveled on the momentum they had built up.

Kean took in each detail as it became clear. First, the tents were not erected. Second, there were men lying around outside the trailers in the heat of the day. Third, not much was left of them after the vultures had dined.

No vultures now. No flesh left to eat. He saw scattered bones. A red cloak, stained brown with blood.

Had he been watching Skyfly, Kean might have marveled at his expertise as he landed the balloon within fifty yards of the trailers, with a bump so slight that although they both fell sideways, they were not hurt.

The scrawny flier was out of the basket fast. He scampered around, accumulating personal possessions first. He piled them up and then threw the covers off the trailers, talking to himself in happy tones as he rummaged through the goods. "What have we here? A set of gears! And excellent plastic tubing. And look here, will you? It just gets better and better!"

He made another pile of larger items from the first trailer and added to it from the second. Gradually, anxiety seemed to come upon him. He began to sort through the larger items again, grumbling to himself.

Kean had done nothing but watch with contempt. Now he went to Skyfly and stood over him. The old man was engrossed in all the goods. "I can't leave *that*," Kean heard him mumble to himself.

The first he knew of Kean's presence was a loud clear voice in his ear.

"Old man."

Skyfly jumped a mile. Kean continued, with soft danger in his voice. "You can't take it all, and you *are* taking me. I don't want you to start thinking otherwise. I'll give you five more minutes, and if you're not done, I'll kill you."

"I can't waste all this!" Skyfly shrieked, in agony at the profit he would lose.

"Then you're dead."

"You won't do anything. You can't fly the balloon without me. You'd die yourself."

Kean took hold of the back of Skyfly's leathery neck and whispered slowly into his ear, with a terrible kind of glee, "I don't care."

Skyfly got the message. He grouched at having to leave so much, and then got happy again about what he had gained. He threw Fireface's cloak around him and twirled in it as though modeling it. He called to Kean, "Isn't it something? Isn't it so *good*?"

He had to hold the cloak in place. The brooch which pinned it was lost somewhere in the dirt. He looked ugly and ridiculous.

Kean walked to the basket. Above it, the floating snakeskin balloon swayed and pulled, as anxious to leave as he was.

Skyfly shouted, "You give me a hand here—we'll be done in half the time!"

Kean leaned on the basket. He was beginning to think it would not give him a moment's concern to have to kill that human vulture over there.

Skyfly read his mind and called, "Don't get superior on me! I got to take what I can—it's how I make my living! We all got to live, don't we?"

Kean tried to think what Hawkerman might require from him and went to examine what was left of the bodies. It did not take a physician's knowledge to conclude that these men had died violently. The body that Kean took to be Fireface's had a deep depression in its skull.

He shouted to Skyfly, "Move yourself. We're going!"

The old man labored hard to fill the basket and was trembling from his exertions by the time they took up their places for flight again. Sneering to himself, still muttering, he unloaded almost all the stones, with Kean's help, and the balloon dragged itself from the dusty ground. Now it was the trading goods and possessions that acted as ballast.

It was hotter than ever, up in the sky. Once he could no longer see all the stuff he had been forced to leave behind, Skyfly became happier, little by little.

"You're a hard man." He grinned at Kean, shaking his head.

Kean despised him. "When will we get back?"

They were traveling high and faster than ever before. "We got good carry from the thermals here," Skyfly said. "If we find some more of these, we could even get back by nightfall. Around this time of year, most of the action goes toward the Big White."

Soon Kean would find out what had happened with, or to, Hawkerman and the others.

Later the thermals were not so helpful, and Skyfly had to use his considerable guile to keep them moving in the direction he wanted. He was getting nervous, Kean saw, and was constantly monitoring the skies.

In the late afternoon, Skyfly grunted with pleasure. "Caught another beauty. This one might get us all the way."

The balloon sailed through the air and Skyfly smiled.

A minute later he said, "I was going to say this was one of the best days of my life."

"And isn't it?" Kean glanced down at his feet. It was almost impossible to move in the basket because of all the odds and ends around them. Dead men's goods.

Skyfly ignored his treasures, gazing back where they had come from. "We got new clouds. One in particular."

Kean searched the skies. By some conjuring trick, the clouds had turned to ragged tufts, not strips, and whiter. Resting on the horizon was a heavier cloud, a kind of pleated mass of vapor, miles away.

It was very far off. Kean said so.

Skyfly said, "It's got a stain on it."

Kean looked intently. There was just a hint of darkness spreading through it, like mud stirring in a waterhole.

"So . . . ," he said slowly.

"So we just hit the Season."

"Oh."

"Put it a different kind of way: in an hour or so, the Season's going to hit us."

❦

In Arcone all maintenance crews were on full alert. The short stubby vanes on the windmills were turning faster than they had for months, and the sensors on top of the Pyramid registered very low atmospheric pressure.

Floors and ceilings were not a priority, and Bonix and his men would act as backup to the exterior maintenance crews if there was damage to Arcone. In high-velocity winds, it took only a small hole in the outer fabric of the Pyramid to produce catastrophe. If the hole widened, the winds would charge in and wreak devastation, lifting whole walls and ceilings.

Disaster like this had not struck in Essa's lifetime, and there was no reason to think it would happen over the coming weeks. She welcomed the drama, all the same. Now her arms were tired from mixing filler, and her mind had gone dumb with the monotony of the work.

She jumped as she heard the sudden movement of the air outside. It sounded like a crowd gasping at a moment of drama in the arena: a sharp inhalation.

The gust whipped onward over the Pyramid. The next one would not be far behind.

This was the Season; it was on its way at last, no doubt about it now. And Arcone was the place to be. She felt sorry for the Wanderers outside the city. It would be awful to be caught in some exposed place at a time like this.

∾

The balloon was traveling faster and faster, as if trying to escape the oncoming cataclysm. Meanwhile, they were being surrounded by clouds of great bulk, rolling in from nowhere and continually redrawing themselves under the influence of the blasting wind. You looked to one side, and the sky had changed; you looked back, and what you had just seen was no longer recognizable.

Kean held onto the basket so tightly that his knuckles hurt.

"You're making good time!" he shouted encouragingly. It was horrific, and yet at the same time, wildly stirring to fly this fast.

"Don't you got brains? This is nothing to do with me!" Skyfly yelled back.

"Can you get us down? Somewhere?"

The wind pulled at Skyfly's face until it looked almost as though he was grinning. "Your man—your Hawkerman— he's killed us!" he shrieked.

The valley was darkening. The rushing air was warm and heavy, and the clouds boiled blacker as the sun set. It was as if they were in the middle of the devil's digestive system, and it had gone very wrong.

With the blackness came terror. The balloon was going so fast, it was well ahead of the basket, trailing it along behind. The gales played spiteful tricks, snatching at them from different angles: the basket heeled over, and trading goods spilled out. A flying piece of metal whirled into the snakeskin envelope and lanced it as if it were a big flying boil.

During this time, the two of them could only hang on with clawed hands and watch. Skyfly had wound some of the leather lines around himself; Kean used strength alone to stop himself from being thrown from the basket.

The winds ceased with shocking suddenness. "Help me! Help me!" Skyfly screamed into the eerie silence, struggling to free himself from the lines. Kean crawled over, falling and rolling on his way to the old man. The sky still boiled; though nearly pitch-dark, it was hotter than ever. Directly above them, the balloon had lost some of its shape.

Kean worked the old man free. Skyfly howled, "We're going down too fast—get rid of it all!" He began to jettison every last precious piece of booty. Kean scrabbled for something heavy and threw out a tungsten drill.

In a minute or so, they would be back on the ground. Then what?

The answer to that was never required. A stormy belch lifted them up again, and in an instant, the winds were back, redoubled in force. The basket shot upward as though it were on a rubber line. Skyfly was crying with fear now.

They soared upward to a towering height, a plaything of the heavens, which cast them down as rapidly as they had been elevated. The emptying balloon descended on them, pressed into the basket by the down-beating wind-storm. Smothered, choking, they saw nothing until it was jerked up again, and they were whipped into the sky once more.

Sheet lightning flashed across the sky, blinding them. When he could see again, Kean realized with horror that they were somewhere above the Gray now and falling again, twisting through the thick air, coming down on the jagged mountain range.

In another flash of lightning, a serrated peak showed to his right, a monstrous edifice that began to tower above them. They were falling into one of the ravines: soon they would be ricocheting to their deaths between the rock faces. Thunder rolled. He felt hands at his throat.

"Altitude!" Skyfly's voice screamed into his ear from behind. "Get out! Get out! I need altitude!"

Strangling Kean with bony hands, Skyfly lurched with him to the lip of the basket. The leaking balloon above them came down again, and they collapsed under a mess of reptile skin and leather lines. Skyfly's hands would not let go of Kean's throat: colors were sparking behind his eyes. He would black out at any moment.

With terror came strength that matched the flier's. Kean bowed his body and rammed his elbows backward. Skyfly let out a gasp, and his hands loosened a little. Kean jerked and rolled them both over, elbowed Skyfly in the face, and hit him again, hard, breaking free of him.

In front of them, a rift ran through the mountain range and cut crossways through the ravine. Acting as a wind tunnel, it channeled a mighty blast of air to throw the balloon back up to where other massive winds grabbed it and threw it sideways. The snakeskin sack snapped upward, as if commanded to stop lazing around, and the balloon was once more flying, after a fashion, as it was designed to.

Kean was alone in the basket. There was no Skyfly. Had he fallen out? Above his head, he caught sight of something swaying.

It was a pair of feet clad in snakeskin.

Skyfly dangled, dead, caught in his precious lines, his neck broken in the instant he was wrenched upward.

The tattered balloon traveled on, a piece of rushing trash in the air. The basket was torn, and one of its plastic supports poked through. Kean grasped onto it and shut his eyes against tiny spears that shot into his face: the first of the rain.

The wind dropped to a simple gale when the rain came, enough to carry the remnants of the balloon onward, upward. Kean lost his sense of time. In each passing second, he was alive, and that was all that mattered. Hold on and be alive while time and space flew by.

As the rain became heavier and more gas left the balloon, the flying machine was inexorably driven lower.

Kean could see nothing through the deluge, until through slitted eyes, he beheld an enormous curved shape coming to fill his vision. It was the apex of a more angular shape, a perfect shape, manmade.

The basket crashed into the top of the Pyramid.

Bouncing and crashing down once more, Kean was pitched out painfully and tumbled down the side of the Pyramid, snatching at the smooth surface for something to hold onto. His legs met an obstruction that diverted him, spinning him around. A section of the clear roofing had buckled under the balloon's first impact; there was a gap, a hole. His legs were through it already, and his momentum carried him sliding after them.

He grabbed for the edge of the buckled panel. It was too thick for his hands to grasp. He had only a fingerhold. The rain washed his grip away, and he fell.

Fell twenty-five yards.

Into the top of a tree.

ELEVEN

People did not shout much in Arcone. At this moment, it seemed that everyone was shouting. With a full maintenance belt strapped to her waist, Essa ran along the corridor behind Bonix and his men. The doors to the Garden were open already, and the work had begun.

Here on the top level of the Pyramid, plant life flourished in this mammoth greenhouse. There were whole acres of creepers and trees and food-bearing vegetation. Tomato plants, olive trees, grape vines, luscious fruits, all too precious to be used as anything except diet additives, although rumor said the Council had a bowl of fruit in the center of their meeting table.

Pacifiers had hauled the mobile maintenance gantry to the split in the roof. There was something sticking through, and men were frantically trying to drag it the rest of the way inside so that they could replace the big panel it had damaged. Another crew was climbing up the side of the

Garden along the supports, going for a smaller area of damage. Bonix ordered Essa to work with this secondary crew.

She climbed up the ladder on the wall, alongside a big tree, to where she could shout at them. "What can I do? Do you need anything?"

There was enough artificial light in here for them to see that it was only an apprentice calling, and one shouted back, "Nothing! Just hope the rain keeps coming, and the winds don't return! Now get out of the way!"

Nice to be wanted. Essa started to climb back down the struts. Branches brushed against her, and she paused to run her hands over the fan-shaped leaves of the giant gingko tree, wonderingly, in admiration of nature's work.

The shouting went on. It was the kind of occasion that demanded a lot of shouting. She reached the bottom, by the roots of the tree. Rain was falling through its leaves. A little distance away was a small clearing where she could watch the first crew on the gantry high above. They sprang back as the obstacle finally came crashing through the roof and jerked to a stop, swinging from side to side, held by strong leather lines. It looked like a big square bucket. There was some immense dark shapeless thing outside on the roofing on the other end of the lines, and it was this that was preventing the bucket from falling. Essa saw that a man was dangling a little way above the bucket, spinning slowly, dressed in outlandish clothes. Rain poured into the garden from the gap in the roof. Soaking wet, the workers had to cut the lines before the man and bucket plummeted to the lush green carpet beneath, ricocheting off branches. The bucket took a big hit and crashed down through the foliage near Essa. Men were rushing to the body. It was an old Wanderer, Essa gathered. Something stirred behind her. She was startled. The sound suggested an animal.

It was—wasn't it? No—it was human, but dressed in leather . . . a young Wanderer lying right by the tree trunk and camouflaged by chance by the brown of the earth at its base. He was extraordinarily pale. There was blood on his head, and now his eyes were opening.

Human eyes. Dazed, lost, and despairing.

This is it. Within the space of two heartbeats, she had decided. If he was found, he would die. If she wanted to rebel against Arcone, there would never again be such an opportunity.

She knelt beside him. "Don't make any noise."

The Wanderer tried to say something and couldn't. Essa was actually laughing. It must be hysteria. If she didn't pull herself together, they were lost. Past the gingko tree and the clearing was an area of dense ferns. She said rapidly, "Trust me. You don't have a choice, anyway. You're not hidden here—they'll find you."

She helped him stand and looked around, fear stabbing at her stomach. No one was looking; too much was going on. There was a lot of excitement about how the old Wanderer's head was nearly severed from his body.

"This way. Quickly," she whispered. They staggered across the clearing, and she helped him crawl underneath the ferns.

"It's going to be all right. I'll help you get out."

Then he spoke, with only his pale hair and face visible to her. A strong face, with steady gray eyes. He said, "How?"

A pale face . . . pale hands, too, she had noticed. Something wrong with one of them . . . one finger too many. Even as she noticed it, the plan was arriving in her mind in nearly every detail.

"Don't worry about how. Worry about keeping out of sight. I'm coming back. I promise. I'll do my best for you."

The girl left Kean's line of vision.

He lay on the soft earth. It smelled so good here. He was going to die. Still going to die, only by different means. Never mind. All he could see was the blur of the fern fronds covering him, nodding into his face. Green heaven. Would it be a slow death? Better not snore, if he fell asleep. He had been awake for days and nights on end, looking back on it. He'd better not snore. Better not sleep at all . . .

He slept.

&

Today Essa was invisible, one hurrying figure among many. Only one Pacifier stopped her. "Where are you going?"

"They need more filler in the Garden."

She would have to get some. It would be her alibi. But she must be so quick—her plan must be carried out before things returned to normal.

Running full-out, she went first to her apartment. It was empty, as she had expected: Marran would have gone to the infirmary, where she was a voluntary nurse when there was an alert. Essa went to her own room. She couldn't risk her brand-new tunic in case Marran noticed its disappearance, but the blue discolored one would do fine—she never wore it, anyway.

She folded it small and stuffed it down the front of the tunic she was wearing, ran out of the apartment—and almost collided with Veramus, of all people.

"What are you doing in the l-living area?"

"I, um—I needed my scalpel—there's a big panic in the Garden."

"I know. I'm g-going there myself."

"Why?"

"I'm making notes for the r-records. This is going to b-be recorded—it's going to be in the b-books! We'll go together, shall we?"

"No. No—I need to get some more filler, too, from the workshop."

"Oh. Couldn't you have picked up a scalpel there?"

"I wanted my own. It's what I'm used to."

His eyes took in the maintenance belt on her waist. She said with a smile, "Look—I've got to hurry."

"Yes—me too."

They ran along to the end of the corridor and went their separate ways, with Veramus calling, "See you there!"

She got a whole pail of filler from the workshop and was halfway out the door by the time she remembered she should account for its absence. She wrote it down on the day sheet while precious time went by, and dashed out again. A Pacifier lifted a hand to stop her as she raced up one of the ramps with the filler. She called, "They need this in the Garden! It's urgent!" and went right on by.

There was a whole squad of Pacifiers on guard at the door to the Garden now. Word of the dead intruder had spread, and security was being stepped up as a small crowd had gathered. Using the pail of filler as her passport, she passed through the gawking bystanders.

Inside the Garden, most of the activity still centered on the big hole, where a new panel had been hoisted. At the side where the smaller hole had occurred, one of the workers was on his way down the ladder by the gingko tree. "What's that?" he asked. "More filler? Good girl. We're doing a patch job for now. That's excellent."

He took the pail. "Should be clear, not white. Never mind. You've done well."

He was back up the ladder immediately to join his fellows. Essa was thankful everyone was so occupied. She went across the clearing to the area of ferns. She had hidden him too well and could not find him for a moment or two.

He was asleep. Of all the nerve. If it had been her, she would have been waiting with fervent gratitude for her savior.

Kean was woken by a hand pressed over his mouth. The girl's face was inches from his own. She had remarkably fierce eyes, dark and deep and passionate. She sounded pretty fierce, too.

"Follow me. Quietly."

He emerged from the ferns and swayed. She grabbed hold of him. "Can you walk? Did you break anything?"

"I don't think so," he said. "Where do we go?"

Essa had taken note of a cluster of bushes nearby. They had interesting berries on them, but at the moment, their appeal was that they were densely clustered. Good cover.

When they got to the bushes, she reached into her tunic and brought out the spare. "Get in there and change."

He hesitated. "Are those girl's clothes?"

"We all wear the same thing here. Bury your own stuff. And be quick."

After giving him some seconds by himself, she entered the bushes. If she was seen standing around doing nothing, it could be dangerous. He was near naked, strapping a knife belt to his pale waist. There was no fat on him; he was as fit as a wild animal.

"Thanks for this," he said, unembarrassed, holding the tunic. "How does it go?"

She pulled it over his head and tugged at it to make it fit better when he had his arms through the sleeves. It was not a ludicrously bad fit, and when it bunched a little as she tied its band on, the knife did not show underneath.

"Thanks," he said again and looked at her. His eyes were still steady, and brighter now; his head was clearing. "Why are you helping me?"

"Because someone had to."

"Well, if you say so. Is everyone here like you?"

"No, they aren't. They'll kill you. Look, we don't have time to talk. I've got to get you nearer ground level. If we can get to the first level, there's a lecture room with windows that open. If it's only raining, we can get you out and you can slide down the side. After that, you're on your own. At least you look like an Arconian. Go on—bury your clothes."

He started to dig with his hands. The soil was soft: dirt from paradise. "What if someone finds them?"

"I don't see why they would. Not for weeks. If I get a chance, I'll take them to the incinerator."

"I'm putting you in danger."

"No—I am. It's my choice." She looked at the gash on his head. "That's going to be useful. All right. Come on, and don't say anything unless you have to."

She took his six-fingered hand and led him out of the bushes, through the clearing, and past the gingko tree. Her hand was warm. Sneaking a glance at her face, he saw she still looked stern.

Following one of the inner paths through the varied vegetation, they came to the tall doors. Four Pacifiers were waiting there. And more outside.

"Pretend you're feeling bad," Essa whispered.

Kean slowed down and let his head roll a little.

"What's your business?" a Pacifier asked.

"Got to get him to the sick bay. He had a fall."

"Can't he go by himself?"

"He's confused. He fell a long way. Could you take him there for me?"

It was a risk, but it worked. "Take him yourself."

Outside the door, Essa saw that the crowd of bystanders had grown. She murmured, "Put your hand on your face. Not that one—keep that one closed."

Kean did so. Now he was leaving the Garden, he did not feel at all safe. Everything was so clean here. And so bright. It was not a place where secrets could be kept for long. He felt ignorant and scared, and he was glad to hang his head and hide behind his good hand.

"Excuse me—got a casualty here," Essa said, and walked through the crowd.

Someone said, "Is it true we've been attacked?"

"No. Well—if we were, it was only by one man. Sorry—I've got to go."

Another voice said, "I'll h-help you."

It was Veramus. He had his scratch tablet at the ready. "He's hurt, is he? What was it? An a-a-accident in service of Arcone? Some n-noble act?"

"Just a fall."

"Can I come and get his s-story?"

"Oh. Aren't you supposed to get permission. I mean—are you allowed to?"

He became anxious at once. "No—I don't know—I'll stay h-here, then."

Good.

But he went on, "I'll j-just come a little of the w-way with you."

And he trotted along beside them, looking inquisitively at Kean. "Who is he? Can't he speak?"

"He's very dazed."

"He's in maintenance?"

"Yes." She had hesitated just too long before answering.

"So what's his n-name?"

"I didn't ask. He's on exteriors—I don't know everyone yet."

"What's your name?" Veramus asked Kean.

Kean made a small groaning noise and pretended to sag at the waist. Essa took hold of him to support him.

So did Veramus, on the other side. They moved on. Kean dragged his feet as realistically as he could. Veramus remarked, "He could get a commendation, if it's a b-bad injury. Oh l-look—he's got a tunic like your old one."

Essa stopped. "Veramus. I think you'd better get back. They'll be bringing a body through soon. A dead Wanderer. Very spectacular, from what I saw of him."

"Oh . . . c-can't m-miss that."

He let them go. Essa thought she felt eyes on her back and could not, just simply could not, resist turning to see if she was right.

She was. Veramus had stayed just where he was, watching them.

Having turned back to him, she had to say something. She called cheerfully, "Let's get together soon, okay?"

He smiled and nodded.

She had to keep going. Would Veramus say anything to anyone? Surely he wouldn't. They were old friends—he couldn't. He might, though . . . She'd get rid of the Wanderer and run back to Veramus and get him to keep his mouth shut. Talk about being impetuous: she was breaking every law in the book. Did a person learn nothing from previous experience?

Other residents of Arcone were anxious about the turmoil in the city.

"What's going on?"

"Where did you come from?"

"Are we being attacked?"

"Has an enemy breached the city?"

All she answered was, "I don't know. Let me pass."

And all the time her companion kept his head down and felt increasingly threatened, increasingly alien. Having realized his ambition to see inside the majestic Pyramid, all he wanted was to get out again in one piece. They were moving so rapidly through the maze of gleaming corridors, it felt like a desperate flight. As an accompaniment, a continuous musical note throbbed and hummed ominously through the whole Pyramid. Essa heard it, too, and was aware of its significance.

At last Kean heard, "In here—quick!" and Essa pulled him into the darkened lecture room.

She ran her hand down the sliding switch by the frame of the door, and small lights glowed like fireflies in the ceiling. Kean was astounded at the size of this room, so orderly with its desks and chairs.

Essa kept the lights low and pulled Kean to one of the windows. "It winds up. You take one handle, I'll take the other."

The panels of the Pyramid overlapped for insulation. Together Kean and Essa pushed the long rectangle up beneath the one above.

Warm air snaked in from the black night. You could tell it was the Season. Only then were the nights less than freezing. Right now there was neither rain nor wind to contend with.

"This is perfect," Essa said. "Just go. You should be all right—let yourself dangle and then slide. After that it's up to you."

Kean got one leg out of the window. "I don't know what to say. I'll do the same for you one day."

"You won't have to. You won't see me again. Just go!"

Kean ducked his head in order to roll out of the window.

The humming sound stopped. All the lights inside Arcone came on at once at full power, and with them all the searchlights that lit the grain fields and the windmills. It was as if white lightning had flashed and frozen at its brightest moment of existence.

Kean felt himself grabbed by Essa. "Get back! You can't make it now!"

He tried to wrench free from her. "I'll run for it."

"No! It's a full stand-by! The field workers will be looking out for intruders! They're armed—there's hundreds of them in the windmills, all watching for anything that moves! You wouldn't make it fifty yards. Get in!"

Kean worked his way back into the lecture room. Taking Essa's example, he wound one of the handles to lower the window back into place. "What should I do, then?"

"I don't know. That noise was the generators. They'd only use this much power if there was a real panic. Everyone's been talking about an attack."

"There's no attack."

"There's you."

"I'm not here to hurt anyone!"

"You're here, though, and they'll kill you."

They stood there in the shining lecture room, talking when there was no time to talk.

Kean said, "Just leave me. Get away from me."

"You're wearing my clothes. If they get you, they'll get me."

"Is there anywhere I can hide?"

"No. Yes. Wait a minute."

Her mind was working again. She grasped his arm without knowing she was doing it.

"There's one place they'd never look. If we could get there. If the maps are right."

TWELVE

They were going up again. It appeared that the Council was indeed suspicious about being attacked; the Pacifiers and first-rank military reserves were all on their way down to ground level.

Kean's strength was returning, and he kept up with Essa with ease. Men passed them, going the other way, some strapping on plastic breastplates as they went, all with the sword every grown man was issued and kept in his living quarters. No one stopped and questioned them; everyone had his own purpose.

Essa's purpose was to reach the Congress Room, situated in the heart of Arcone. It was all quite clear on the maintenance master plan: there was a cavity wall running around three sides of the room, packed with lightweight padding to kill all sounds. The fourth wall was one of the massive supports for the floor of the Measureless Chamber. Essa wanted to get to a corner where the rigid buttress met the flimsier materials.

They would be in a dead end there, which terrified her—and first they had to get by the door to the Congress Room itself, which was set back from the corridor in a little vestibule, where a guard was stationed night and day.

As they passed him, the Pacifier at the door saw the dried blood on Kean's head and stepped forward.

"Stop."

"Can I help you?" Essa asked, with her heart trying to hammer its way out of her chest.

"Why is he hurt? Is there fighting below?"

"No. No . . . some panic, that's all. A man ran amok."

"Where are you going? What's your trade?"

"Maintenance. He's a nursing orderly—tried to break up the fight—now we've been called to the Garden. What a night!"

"Can't he speak for himself?"

Kean snapped, "We have work to do," and prayed the man wouldn't ask for details.

"I wish I was down there," the Pacifier growled. "I'd sort things out quick enough."

"We all have our own responsibilities," Essa said sententiously.

"Now if you don't mind . . . ?" Kean asked, suppressing a very real impatience.

"Proceed."

They ran onward. Now came the critical moment: the turn into the dead end. Was the Pacifier watching?

Essa looked. He was back at his post in the vestibule. She pulled Kean sideways into the short corridor.

How much time did they have before someone else came along the main corridor? Did the Pacifier patrol the walls of the Congress Room?

"This is it," Essa whispered. "You keep watch."

She pulled out her scalpel. Her fingers were fluttering with nerves, disobedient just when she needed all her skill. She drew the blade down the corner where the wall met the solid support. It sliced through in a perfect straight line, to her great relief. Next she cut a line at a right angle where the soft wall met the flooring, creating a flap she could bend and lift.

Carefully. There couldn't be any tears. It was one thing to repair a clean cut; ragged edges were another matter. Meanwhile someone was going to pass and see them, and within hours she might find herself caged above the reservoir, waiting to be lowered into the water.

It would come up over her head. She would grip the bars, climbing to the roof of the cage. Her mouth would break through the surface of the water. She would take her last frantic breaths before she went under for the last time . . . Think of something else.

"What are you called?" she asked Kean in a low voice.

"Kean."

"You get in here, Kean, and you hide till I can get back to you. I have to seal you in, but you can cut your way out if you have to. You've got a knife."

He didn't like the idea. You could see it in his face. She knelt on the floor, raising the neat flap she had created. "It's the best I can do. It's actually a really big space—you'll be all right. But you have to hurry."

Kean got down on his hands and knees and looked in. Loose padding, plastic that had degenerated into a fuzzy gray substance, was drooping out from the cut wall already. At least it was loose—he could get in. He did, worming his way into the narrow space. It was about two yards across before he touched the far wall. He could move the plastic stuff easily and make room for himself. But it was going to be claustrophobic.

He wriggled around forty-five degrees, and the girl's face was right by his as she stuffed the padding back into the wall cavity. Why had she done this for him? What was in it for her? Who was she, anyway?

"What's your name?" he said, too loudly.

"Essa."

"When will you come back?"

"When I can."

She stood, and all he saw were her legs. They were attractive legs. She had not seemed at all upset by his abnormal hand . . . and now he was going to be so trapped in here . . .

Essa spread the filler with practiced skill and worked it down with the scalpel. Would there be enough? It was a lot to ask of the small amount she carried in her work belt. She was going to run out too soon, wasn't she? And how long did it actually take to drown? Would it be easier to embrace your death and let the water into your lungs immediately?

The vertical line was sealed. Now for the one at floor level. *Thank you, thank you.* There would be enough filler. Barely.

It got very dark in the cavity where Kean lay. It was like being buried. He took slow, calming breaths and suddenly felt an irresistible urge to push the padding farther away from his face.

Holding the woolly gray substance away from his mouth, he took some more long, deep breaths. He couldn't stay here long. He would be screaming to be let out within an hour.

One breath at a time. Get a rhythm going . . .

Outside, Essa finished repairing the wall. Next she had to get out of the little dead end without the Pacifier getting sight of her crossing the corridor . . . He was safely inside the vestibule. She was running again, trying to keep her footsteps light. Where was Veramus now? That was the question. At times of crisis, his duties were as a messenger—in a full stand-by, the most likely place for him to be was down in the main lobby awaiting instructions. With every second that passed, danger pressed more strongly. Her place was in the Garden, and here she was, going in the opposite direction. The passageways were deserted now. Everyone was where they should be, except her. She felt terribly conspicuous. Prompted by hope more than reason, she made a detour to look in on the History workshop. If Veramus was in there, it would be so much easier . . .

It was empty. All she had accomplished was to waste more precious minutes.

When at last she came down to the point where the main corridor met the big lobby, the statues were looking down approvingly on the might of Arcone assembled in full, glaring electric light. She had not been thinking straight: there was no crowd gathered here in which she might disguise her presence, only the imposing ranks of Pacifiers, a small cluster of messengers, and a group standing aside, talking in animated tones.

She kept close to the wall, not wishing to be seen. It took only a quick inspection of the messengers to see that Veramus was not among them, so there was no point hanging around to become the target of questions. She had no choice: she would have to dash back up to the Garden without finding him, unless by glorious chance she came across him on the way. Even if she didn't find him, surely he wouldn't say anything until after they had spoken together—their friendship must mean *something* to him.

She turned away and heard his voice at the same time.

Veramus called in a shrill voice, "There she is! Get her! Ask her! I'm telling you the truth!"

In his act of betrayal, she didn't hear even the merest suggestion of a stammer. Grollat stepped forward from where he stood with the boy who had been her friend, and his somber eyes met Essa's and held them.

He said heavily, "Elessa. Stay very still."

⌒

Panic charged into Kean as he woke. Where was he? What was this material pressing down on his face? Who was talking?

He had slept again. He felt strong. He was lying between two walls right in the middle of the Pyramid. He did not like the Pyramid. He had been crazy to ever think that this was where he belonged.

The voices again. Now someone was shouting. It was funny how much effort the man was putting into it, only to sound weak and small from where Kean lay. He could hardly hear what the words were.

"I acted in the interests of Arcone! What is the word of a Wanderer worth? Do we entrust our security entirely to Dagman, or do we take sensible measures when danger threatens?"

The voice that answered was low, and the argument it carried was more measured. This was so frustrating: Kean wanted to hear more. Dagman? Why would Dagman have any say in the affairs of the pyramid city?

Burrowing through the insulating material, he reached the far wall. The voices were clearer here but not clear enough.

His knife. He would be taking a terrible chance. He took it from under the tunic he wore. The girl's tunic. Essa's. What had happened to her? Was she waiting for her moment, or was she in trouble, unable to get to him? And if he used the knife and was discovered here, what harm might he bring to her? He *had* to hear, though. Had to.

The knife was whetted as sharp as any scalpel. Where should he cut?

Low down. Not too low down. He wanted to be able to see as well as hear.

He cleared himself a space by the wall and lay down, resting on one elbow. The wall was about a quarter inch thick. He set the point of the knife on it and pushed, slowly increasing the pressure. After a short space of time, the wall gave up its resistance in a rush, and he had a moment's horror that the blade would shoot through several inches.

He sliced downward a little way and then across, making a tiny version of the flap Essa had cut. He bent back the flap and inched closer to the wall.

Listen first. An old man was speaking in a voice that had a rustling, papery quality.

"With all respect, may I point out that it has always been the aim of the Council to *agree* on decisions. In order to do that, we must be consulted."

The next voice that spoke was richer and younger—the man who had been shouting loud enough to wake Kean.

"My dear Nastor, an eminent historian such as yourself has a finely developed gift for wordplay. Might I point out, equally respectfully, that in times of peril, the Prime Conscience is empowered to take decisions for the good of Arcone. I am the Prime Conscience, and that is what I did."

The old voice said, "In this case, there was no need for sudden action—that is all I am saying. The waste of energy was morally wrong. There was time to convene the Council first."

"The Season will replenish stocks very fast. The windmills are already hard at work. That is not the issue. You call into question my judgment in declaring an emergency, and I ask you this: do you really think that when danger threatens, our first duty is to have interminable arguments like this one?"

"Danger did not threaten."

"I disagree. Danger did *threaten*, it's just that it did not *happen*."

"And now it is you who are playing with words."

Another voice came in. "What is your opinion, Commander? As a military man?"

A silence. An attentive silence. The voice that spoke next was deep, and reverberated through the chamber, although the man talked quietly.

"It does no harm to remind the people that they may have to fight for their way of life. A general alert was certainly called for. I would have kept the lights low, drawn in any attackers, and butchered the lot of them. Since you ask."

The Prime Conscience was triumphant. "And is that what you all want? Killing? A general bloodletting in which our own citizens might die? Do you want to start a war? Is that what you want?"

The deep voice spoiled his moment for him. "Can we move onto the realities of the situation? There was no attack. Our preventative measures ensured there was no attack. There was a moment of alarm. The city went on alert, but now we know there were two intruders only."

Nastor said quickly, "The girl must be purified, of course. Are we agreed?"

She had been caught, then. A pause. Kean imagined a show of hands taking place. But what was purification?

He heard the Prime Conscience announce dryly, "Well, we are at least agreed on that."

"You had knowledge of her, Commander," Nastor said. "You disciplined her previously."

"I did."

"You were not hard enough on her, it seems."

"I could hardly demand her death for a minor transgression."

"Had you done so, we might not now have an interloper in the city."

"It amuses me," said the Commander, unamused, "how the timid are always so anxious to kill people. The punishment must fit the crime. The girl is now going to die; be satisfied with that."

Kean thought, *Because of me, they're going to kill her.*

"And what of the intruder? Where is he?"

"She claims she doesn't know. She says she directed him back up to the Garden. What we know of their movements seems to confirm that, and it is probably the only place in which concealment is feasible for any length of time. It's even possible he got out."

"Do you believe she's being truthful when she speaks?"

"It's hard to tell when someone is so frightened. And before you call for torture, Nastor, I'd remind you it is not the Arconian way. She will have several days now to consider her situation. Time to repent and confess."

The Prime Conscience concurred. "The laws must be obeyed. Without wishing to congratulate myself, I can only say that her behavior appears to vindicate actions I took many years ago. Bad blood in her veins, Commander, and bad blood will out."

Kean began to make the hole bigger. He just had to see, now.

Yet another voice came in. "Were these men sent to spy? Did they have a reason to infiltrate our city?"

"They didn't infiltrate it; they crashed into it," the Commander said. You could hear his patience wearing thin. "It's windy out there. You might have noticed."

"The Wanderer must be found."

"If he's still here, he will be."

At last, Kean had a view. It was infuriatingly restricted, but he could see part of a long low table. The Prime Conscience was speaking again. Kean couldn't see him, but he could see the old man—Nastor—and the Commander, and another man's back on this side of the meeting table.

The Prime Conscience's voice: "I have a proposal for the Commander."

The Commander was a dark, big man. Nastor was much fatter than his small voice had suggested, with wisps of hair trained over his balding head. There was a bowl of bright foodstuffs on the table, colored in reds and greens: plants of some kind.

The Commander reached out for a red fruit. "What is your proposal, Prime Conscience?" he said politely, and bit into the fruit. Juice ran down his chin.

"You will visit Dagman at once, ask him what he knows of this."

Kean waited, so still that he was part of the wall.

THIRTEEN

The Commander considered the proposition.

He said softly, "Very well. If that is what the Council wishes."

"Can we agree on that?" The Prime Conscience asked with a trace of irony. Nastor nodded, and others must have, too. "So, is our business concluded?"

Nastor had the last word. "We will meet tomorrow, Prime Conscience?"

"We will, Nastor—we will meet as often as you like!"

The humor went down well, and the meeting seemed to break up with smiles. Chairs were pushed back, and men filed from the room, going to Kean's left. When people stood up, he could not see their heads, only their bodies. One of the headless bodies paused.

"Prime Conscience, I would be honored if you would take water with me."

"I thank you, Auramas, but it is late, and I wish to speak to the Commander before I retire."

"You will remember we have a cup to share at some time?"

"I look forward to it, Auramas."

"May your sleep be untroubled, Prime Conscience."

"And yours."

The Commander had not moved from where he sat. He was now casually eating another of the red fruits. When everyone had gone, the Prime Conscience came to sit beside him. He was younger than Kean had imagined, muscular, with a deep cleft of concentration running between his brows. He said good-naturedly, "Don't eat all the tomatoes."

"It's the only good reason for coming here," the Commander said with similar easy humor.

The Prime Conscience reached out and took one of the small green fruits. They ate in silence for a moment.

"That fool Nastor wanted to use this as an excuse to withhold deliveries for the coming year," the Prime Conscience said wearily, "until we had many proofs of Dagman's good faith."

"Nastor looks for conspiracies everywhere because he is dishonest himself."

"Nevertheless, do you not think we might take advantage of this accident—if that is what it was?"

"How take advantage?"

"You could put it to Dagman that Wanderers had intruded—that he had failed us. Renegotiate to a point below the ten percent."

"You said yourself, it was an accident. Leave it, Maxamar. Ten percent is nothing."

"It would be a coup for me—to reduce the payment."

"Your reputation stands high enough already. The arrangement has worked well for a long time. Leave it alone."

"Well . . . all right." His regret was plain. "And what if you find that Dagman is losing his hold—what then?"

"Immediate punitive measures will be taken. It has been many years since they felt the full power of Arcone."

"A little bloodletting? Some executions?"

"A lot of bloodletting. A lesson that will last."

"In history, it was a regular event," the Prime Conscience said reasonably.

"I could guarantee you an event that would put us all on some tapestry or another."

"You sound contemptuous, Commander."

"Do I, Prime Conscience? I'm sorry."

Maxamar said thoughtfully, "Tomorrow Nastor will plead for advancement for young Veramus. He wants more historians on the Council, especially those who might be easily led."

"Refuse him."

"It would be hard. The boy acted well. He could be given something."

"Give him nothing. He acted for himself alone. As does Nastor. Whatever anyone might say about you, Prime Conscience, you think first of Arcone and only then of yourself."

"To me, they are the same thing."

"That is, of course, your greatest strength—your undeviating self-admiration."

It was said quite straight, but the Prime Conscience roared with laughter. "Oh, Grollat. What would I do without you? It is you who are the conscience of Arcone—not I!"

"Now that, Maxamar, is something I have no desire to be."

The Prime Conscience got up. "You will leave at once for the Lakes?"

"I'll go straight from here."

"Good. May your sleep be untroubled. If you get any!"

The Prime Conscience laughed again and clapped the Commander on the shoulder as he got up from the table. He passed from Kean's view.

The Commander ate steadily. He did not look like a man who got much sleep at all, let alone the untroubled variety. Under his hooded lids, his eyes were dark and deep.

He stood, dropped the last tomato back into the bowl unfinished, and walked to the door. The lights went dim. Something was odd; he had not left the room. Now he crossed Kean's vantage point going the other way. Going where?

Kean heard something scraping across the floor . . . and then back again . . . and then all was quiet.

The Commander. Dagman. A deal. What should he do? The girl wasn't coming back. They were going to kill her, but not yet. There was nothing he could do for her by himself . . . there were, in fact, no choices to make, and time was passing already.

Taking a firm hold on his knife, he widened the tiny hole he had been looking through. Then he sliced down right through the wall into the darkened Congress Room. The room was hung with tapestries, and the long table in the center could seat some twenty men. None of this interested Kean, who went swiftly in the direction Grollat had taken. Here a very large tapestry depicting the Pyramid itself, white under a benign blue sky, hung all the way to the floor.

He pushed the tapestry aside and was at first disappointed. There was only a blank wall behind it. And this wall had a structural purpose; it was feet thick, infinitely more solid than the one his knife had cut so easily. His hand explored the wall's surface. A crack ran down it, and by the crack was a molded ridge: a near-invisible handle. He tugged and the concealed door slid open.

Instantly he heard footsteps going down, a long way below him. He went through the door, shut it quietly, and let the tapestry fall back into place. Coming out of an embrasure, he stood on a little landing facing a metal spiral staircase. Above him was the weight of the Measureless Chamber; below him the staircase descended through the gargantuan buttress as far as the eye could see. Grollat's footwear was metal-shod, and from the sound of it, he had already traveled a long way down. Kean started after him.

Before his eyesight adjusted to the darkness, he went slowly, and still managed to bump into the handrail. It took time to get used to the tight spiral of the stairs. His bare feet made no sound on them, and after a while he could go faster and more surely.

At intervals of many yards, he came upon other doors that would open into other areas of the Pyramid. Finally the noise of Grollat's footsteps stopped, and light flowed up the stairwell. He had left the stairs.

Kean went down even faster. He couldn't lose him now. He discovered he could take two steps at a time, landing so softly on each tread that it was like flying. The light got closer. Another of the doorways. Open. He was going to go through it when he heard sounds suggesting someone on the other side had the same intention. Kean darted behind the open door and flattened himself against rock.

Fortunately Grollat was in a hurry. He came out fast, slammed the door behind him without spotting Kean in the darkness, and went on down the stairs.

He wore a dark hooded cloak.

He was the man in the shadows in Dagman's dwelling.

Kean could not follow at once, so he filled the time by trying the handle on the door. It opened under his touch . . . He couldn't resist it.

A bedchamber. Not very clean. Grollat's uniform lying on a narrow pallet. Little else in the room but a chest and table, and a pitcher of water. No windows, but another open door revealed a chamber beyond the bedroom. Kean raised the pitcher to his mouth and drank long and deeply. It was the purest substance he had ever tasted, and he set it down again with reverence before he went into the main room of Grollat's apartment, where there was a long narrow window with a view of the marvel of the underground reservoir.

He couldn't stay long. He went to one side of the window and looked through. Movement at once drew his gaze downward. Men were working sluice gates to channel the rising water to where it was needed. Even this soon in the Season, the reservoir was filling appreciably. His eye followed some steps leading upward. He saw a metal cage, miniature from here, hanging from the rounded ceiling. A tiny form sat in the cage, arms on upraised knees, chin resting on arms, hair falling down around its face. Long dark hair.

The cavern swarmed with Water Workers and Pacifiers; there was nothing he could do for her, and the Commander would by now have gone some distance.

Back in the stairwell, he was relieved to hear Grollat's footsteps still going down. Taking two steps at a time, Kean cut the space between them. When the footsteps stopped, Kean did, too.

This time when Grollat opened a door, no light poured through. Kean heard the door close with a clang, and ran down the last of the stairs. He had to locate the door handle by touch alone. It was pitch-black down here. When he found the handle, it was rusty. Even the stairs were rusty here. Water entered this place on occasion.

He waited for many seconds, counting to himself. He could not afford to let Grollat hear him coming. When he tried the door, it took a lot of strength to drag it open. He did not shut it fully, afraid of the noise it would make.

He stood on a narrow stone pathway above . . . above what? It was a nightmare, being so uncertain of what was around him and below him. The wall began to curve outward at head height, so he was near the top of wherever he was . . . and he knew where to go next. Ahead of him, a speck of light wavered far down the walkway. Grollat was a fit man, and he was hurrying. Kean began to follow the light, keeping one hand against the inner wall for balance. Once his foot dislodged a pebble, and he heard it hit stone not very far below him. After that he was able to move faster, traveling into an unknown which was at least not bottomless.

∽

Grollat's interrogation after her capture had been, well, odd. With two Pacifiers standing behind her as if she was savagely wild and dangerous, they had faced each other across a table in a brightly lit holding cell near the Armory.

He asked the questions with a suggestion of a sigh in his voice, as if it was all meaningless but he had to do it anyway, as a matter of routine.

"Where is the Wanderer?" That was the question he asked most.

So they hadn't found him. The answer she gave, over and over, both to this and to other questions, was "I don't know." She said this when he asked why she had aided an enemy of

Arcone. She said it when he asked what had gone through her head when she found the young man.

Some questions she answered truthfully, because what was the point of lying? The intruder was young, yes . . . Not armed, except for a knife . . . No, he had not threatened her . . . If he had a reason for being in Arcone, he had not told her what it was.

The Commander asked one more time, "Where is he?" and she answered, "I don't know," one more time, and then he dismissed the guards.

She suspected he wanted to talk to her more personally, and when he didn't say anything, the silence made her start talking instead.

She found herself saying, "I've let you down. I'm sorry."

He shrugged. "It's not important. I didn't expect anything of you, so I can't be disappointed in you."

"You gave me a chance, though."

"And you acted according to your nature. Should I be surprised at that?"

"I still don't know why I did it. I just couldn't stop myself."

"It's hard to think of consequences sometimes. To believe in them."

"I'm really going to be drowned, though, aren't I?"

"Yes. There's nothing I can do about it."

"You've been kind. I don't understand why."

He made a wry grimace. "Looking at it now, it seems you were always going to destroy yourself, one way or another. 'When' was the only question. It's fate, isn't it? I thought

I saw in you an individual who could make a difference . . ." He leaned forward, his eyes coming alive. "Perhaps you have made a difference. Perhaps this is what I wanted."

She made a weak joke. "I wouldn't have made you Commander of the Pacifiers. You don't really seem to fit the job."

Grollat leaned back again. "I actively pursued the post. The Commander has the freedom to leave the city, to see the greater world outside." He examined one of his big, dirty, hairy hands. "I had a daughter—we had a daughter. She was born without the gift of speech. She had no tongue. We gave her up. She was expelled. Five years old. It was the correct thing to do."

Essa blurted out, "I couldn't have done that."

He was not insulted. "I think we have already established that you never know *what* you are going to do. Anyway, we thought—my wife and me—that we had come to terms with what we had done. But the pain grew more, not less. I wanted to know what had happened to our child. To do that, I had to be able to talk to the Wanderers."

"And you did?"

"After I became Commander."

"And is she alive? Do you know?"

Grollat said, "It took me a long time to achieve this rank. When, finally, I came upon information about our daughter, it was to find that she died only months after we abandoned her." Then he said, "Do you understand what I mean about fate, now?"

"No."

"Wishing changes nothing. We are defined by our actions, not our hopes, and in all our actions, we have far less choice than we like to think. Some things are set, waiting to happen, and we don't change them. Can't change them."

"What a depressing idea."

"Yes," he agreed. "Isn't it?" He added lightly, "There is much about you that is admirable. Refreshing. I like talking to you."

"I'm going to die," Essa said with a pang of terrible fear.

As she said it, she saw that the thought did not disturb him, and the moment of intimacy vanished. They both knew it. He said in an official kind of way, "I will see you again, if I can."

And they talked about how she was allowed visitors. About how she would not be lowered into the water until the Season had filled the reservoir. That was the tradition at this time of year. The end of their conversation had been rational, practical. Unreal. Men would condemn her to violent death; would work the machinery that would ensure it; would watch the waters close over the top of the cage and wait; would see the cage raised, with her dead in it; would walk away congratulating themselves on a job well done.

Now Essa could see those black waters far beneath her. She could easily see all around, because the bars of the fifteen-foot cage were widely spaced. Everything she touched was metal: it was difficult to get comfortable in any position for any length of time. Looking through the bars of the base, through which she could easily slip her legs, it seemed a whole mile down to the reservoir from up here. It was the height that was the scary thing. The water itself had a calming effect, strangely. It was still and cool and impersonal; she liked the way it made ripples of light appear on the shiny ceiling so close above. Just overhead, on the ground floor of the Pyramid, was the central cooling system. At this time of year, it was less active, although the temperature so near to it was still distinctly chilly.

When the workers released some of the water into conduits feeding various parts of Arcone, the surface of the reservoir took on lazy movement. The water was a magical substance, and Veramus's desire to write poetry about it was quite understandable. His betrayal was quite understandable, too, if you knew him like Essa did.

No one had visited her, not even Bonix or Marran. They would be scared, already tainted by their association with her. However, she was not quite alone, for set into the walls on one side of her were the Self-Examination Cells, and at present their occupants were not so much examining themselves as examining her. No doubt they felt comparatively comfortable about their own circumstances when they thought about her plight. *Elessa . . . Always acted on impulse, and now she's going to die because of it.*

Impulse. Or was it fate, as Grollat had suggested? At the time she had indeed felt, for a moment, that destiny had brought her together with the Wanderer. She'd felt a kind of instant connection with him.

She could see the Commander's narrow window across the cavern from her. It reflected the light, and you couldn't see in. On his orders, a Pacifier now patrolled along the ledge that supported the Self-Examination Cells. Her own personal warder, full of self-importance—and her food. He pulled in her cage to serve it, and he ate her leftovers when she was done. He'd get fat at this rate; she'd hardly been able to swallow a single mouthful.

They still hadn't caught the Wanderer as far as she knew. He might still be where she had left him, stuck between the two walls, waiting for her. He would starve to death. But there was something about him, wasn't there? Maybe he would escape. If he did, he would turn his back on Arcone and her without a second glance. Well, all along it had been like setting a wild animal free. You did not expect gratitude.

She looked down through the bars again. The water was such a beautiful substance. Perhaps it wouldn't be too terrible when it happened.

FOURTEEN

Kean had lost all sense of time in the darkness, jogging onward after the pinprick of light. It was painful when his bare feet came down on the rocky ledge. It no longer mattered what noise he made: above him there was now a continuous pounding of sound that could be felt all the way through the rock. He guessed it was raining up on the surface, one of those near-solid deluges that flattened and destroyed so much of the valley's plant life.

He must have traveled a whole mile already. It seemed the tunnel could go on forever. The girl who had helped him came into his mind. It was unreasonable, but he felt bad about leaving her to her fate back there. He began to think of arguments in his favor. He hadn't asked for her help. She would have had her own reasons for doing what she had done. In a way, it was none of his business. She must surely *know* he couldn't possibly do anything to help her . . . The more good reasons he found for not feeling guilty, the guiltier he felt. It made him angry. He hadn't even thanked her, not really, had he? Well, he had in a way. He had thanked her for the clothes, anyway—he remembered that. Oh. And he had said, "I'll do the same for you one day." Well . . . she must have understood it was just something you say. All the same, he wished he hadn't said it, or hadn't remembered saying it. She couldn't expect him to do anything for her. What could he do? It was just one of those things, and anyway, your only loyalty was to your team; you didn't do things for strangers. His thanks to her would be to get away, because that was what she had wanted for him, after all.

Follow the speck of light down the infinite tunnel, that was all he could do. Feeling so *angry*.

∽

Kean stumbled along in perpetual darkness, and Essa was trapped in perpetual light, and neither had any idea that dawn was approaching.

A visitor came to Essa.

Marran.

The guard pulled the cage to the side of the cavern and let her in before easing the hanging prison back into place. When they embraced, awkwardly, the cage swayed.

Marran said, "Your father wouldn't come."

"Oh well."

"He couldn't. It hurts him so much. Maybe not all of it for the right reasons, but he does care, Elessa."

"If you say so."

Marran began to cry. "This is all my fault!"

"No—no." Essa held her and comforted her. The cage shifted as they clung together, with Essa giving Marran little pats on her back.

This is strange. I'm the one who's going to die.

She heard herself saying softly, "It's all right. It's all right."

Marran disengaged herself and regained some control. "We should have been open with you. We only wanted to spare you pain. It doesn't mean you weren't loved."

Essa said, "I'm not dead yet. Don't talk like that."

"I did wonder sometimes if I really loved you. Now I know."

"I wasn't a good daughter. I'm sorry. I've brought trouble to you."

"What does that matter?" Marran smiled bravely. "I was storing up trouble for myself, anyway. After they had taken you, they searched our apartment. They found some pictures I keep hidden. Ones that are not correct."

"You? You concealing subversive art?" Essa was incredulous.

"Oh—I'm in no great danger. Unless you count losing some status. Your father worries a lot about demotion—but I know he worries for you, too. He won't talk about it, but he does."

"But he isn't my father."

"No," Marran said reluctantly. "The Commander told you." She became angry. "It wasn't his place to!"

"Did you know my parents?"

The anger dwindled. "No. I'm sorry."

She told Essa how her true mother and father had been people of privilege at a time when Bonix and Marran were residents of low status. "When we took you in, I thought we were simply wishing to do a correct thing. And—yes— hoping to gain advancement . . . that, too. Later I knew I had always wanted a child. It's only now I know that the child I wanted was you."

There were more hugs and more tears from Marran. It was like being with another person, a person Essa did not know at all. *It's all too late. Now it doesn't mean anything.*

"Have you seen Veramus?" she asked.

Marran said vehemently, "Not once—and if he's avoid- ing me, he knows what's good for him. I'd like to kill him."

"It's not his fault, Marran—there are hundreds just like him. You'd have a lot of killing to do once you started."

Marran said bitterly, "There's one of them now."

Essa looked down and saw that Maxamar had swept into the cavern with an entourage of prominent citizens. He had come to praise the Water Workers and encourage them in their work as it grew ever more arduous.

"The Prime Conscience?" Essa said.

"He was the one who reported your mother and father to the Council. So Veramus had a fine example to follow."

"Maxamar did that?"

"When he was younger, he and your parents were friends."

Essa could not get angry about it. She was a prisoner awaiting execution. Those with lives to live could get worked up about the unfairness of life in Arcone; it was no longer her concern.

Marran wanted to know, "Do you forgive me?"

"What for?"

The older woman was nonplussed. "I'm not sure."

"It was all my own doing. I wish I could find someone to blame, but I can't. You've never done me any harm." She wished Marran would go, leaving her to contemplate the water again.

Her adoptive mother talked rapidly before their time together concluded. She was petitioning the Council on Essa's behalf. "Believe me, Elessa—there is still hope."

No. I won't hope. I won't dream of a future. There isn't one.

They hugged a last time before the cage was swung back to let Marran out. "There is always a chance," Marran said fervently. "Always. I won't allow you to die like this."

They wouldn't listen to a mother's emotional pleading. The laws of Arcone were implacable to those who strayed.

Essa said with a crooked smile, "It's only water. It won't hurt."

⁓

The dot of light wavered and vanished.

Clinging to the wall, Kean kept going. It was becoming easier. He had been traveling by touch alone for so long that at first it seemed an illusion when the blackness relaxed its hold. Nearing the place where the torch had disappeared, he became surer that natural light was filtering into the subterranean shaft from somewhere ahead.

When he could make out his surroundings, the unfathomable tunnel shrank to its true size. Not big at all. Thirty yards or so in diameter, it was a natural fault running through the substrata, one that had been artificially enhanced where necessary. At its lowest level, below the ledge he moved along, was a sheen of algae.

It was a water conduit. A giant water pipe. All but dry at present.

He hurried on much faster.

The tunnel was opening out into a large underground basin half full of water. There was one big shaft that opened out right over the basin, and while most of the light filtered down through this, the general obscurity was lifted in other areas of the basin, too, for above the water were the mouths of other smaller tunnels. The general pattern indicated that there were more shafts lower down: it was like being in a stony heart served by pipes and arteries. Instead of blood, the upper orifices dripped down rainwater.

When Kean refocused on the task at hand, he found he had lost all sense of where the Commander had gone. He put out a hand to steady himself, and it touched something metal. A ladder. Leading up at an angle into a hole that was definitely manmade, although no illumination came down it . . . Well, the path had ended: while the basin extended well beyond the ladder, this seemed to be the only exit, so

Grollat had gone this way, and this was the way he would go, too.

He climbed the ladder. Soon rock enclosed him in a narrow funnel. He went upward, hand over hand, until his head bumped into something wooden.

A trapdoor. Now what? No telling what was up there . . . or who.

There was no sound. Of that he was sure. He pushed at the wood, and it moved. He listened again. Nothing. He pushed harder, and it lifted clear a few inches. Weighed down by something, though . . .

Still no sound. He forced the trapdoor up and to one side, and an animal slid across his view. An empty animal, it was—just its skin. There was light up there, and you could tell it was artificial light, because the color was so deep and rich.

No one shouted, nothing moved up there. He inched upward and looked. He was staring at an interior that seemed familiar. There were more skins—there were animal skins everywhere—and a lamp burned in one corner.

It was Dagman's inner room. He wasn't here, but you could smell him. Not the place to be. Kean would never get out of the building. It was the very center of Cruiser power.

He went down the ladder again, replacing the trapdoor over his head as best he could. Back in the big basin, it was a question of finding another exit to take, once his eyes had again adjusted to the dimness. There were none that he could see. However, if he could somehow reach the nearest tunnel that showed light above the basin . . . It wasn't very far away from where he stood at the end of the path.

No one in the valley could swim: there was nothing to swim in. He reached a foot down into the water. Pushed it down farther till he nearly lost his balance. Ah—there . . . a kind of fold in the rock formation . . . one that could provide a foothold. He lowered himself slowly into the water. It was cold, and the novelty of it was terrifying. There were lumps and bumps to hold onto with his hands . . . that little fold supported his feet . . .

The slipperiness of the rock was like a layer of grease. As soon as he let go of one handhold to seek another, his foot shot downward, and he lost his grip and went under. In a complete panic, he threshed his arms and legs, and took mouthfuls of water. Fortunately the Bleacher clothes were light, and at last, spluttering and wanting to cry out in his terror, he broke the surface again. He had traveled in his struggles. His thrashing hands met the opening of a tunnel mouth, and he grabbed at it. Wet and shaking as he was, it took all his strength to drag himself out of the water. His feet continued to slip; it was only by frantic scrabbling that he was able to get an elbow into the tunnel and then throw his shoulder after it.

Pitch-blackness again. In the state of mind he was in, Kean did not read the message this might have given him. He hauled himself into the tunnel face first and squirmed onto his back in order to get his legs in. One last effort, and he had gotten all of his body into the tunnel. Unfortunately he continued to move even after his muscles stopped work-ing, for the tunnel did the exact opposite of what Kean had hoped—it traveled down. He was sliding on his back, not fast, yet powerless to stop himself in the clammy smooth-ness of the shaft. He writhed onto his front again; he was sliding down face forward into water—more water—shooting under . . . coming to a halt, wholly submerged. Panic set in all over again until he realized that this time he was touching the bottom. He came up onto his knees, and in attempting to stand, banged his head on rock. He was crouched in water which was less than waist height.

The shaft of the little well rose straight up above him, narrow, with a small gray circle marking daylight at the top. How far up? Hard to tell. There was no question of going back, anyway, so what difference did it make? The walls were damp and dangerous, but if he stood and forced himself just a little way up the shaft, he could climb the rest of the way by using his feet against one side and his back against the other.

After what he had been through in the last few minutes, this was relatively straightforward once he had drawn him-self up out of the water. Then it was a matter of obstinate, uncomfortable labor. He had ascended only halfway before his shoulders and legs were hurting badly, and there was an insistent pain in his lower back.

Thoughts jostled for his attention. What time of day was it? How far away from Dagman's house would he be when he got out? Was he going to emerge in the sight of Cruisers?

If this well was still working, wouldn't it be guarded? Oh—it must have stopped raining suddenly. No droplets were falling down the well. And there was no sound of wind, either. So, a lull up top. That was bad news. His best chance of getting out of Cruiser territory was if everyone had taken cover.

Somehow he had to get to Hawkerman. If he could find him. There was much to report.

And then, when he was almost at the top of the well, he heard a voice coming from above, and although it was so faint that it was almost inaudible, Kean half believed it was Hawkerman's voice.

"Waiting . . . nothing better to do."

The flat tone was just like Hawkerman's.

"Back off." The man repeated himself more loudly. "I said *back off.* You want him dead? That suits me fine, because I do, too."

It was Hawkerman.

His voice came again. "Now—you go back in and get Dagman out. I don't talk to you, Frumitch—only Dagman."

The well was harder to climb near the top. Wider. Kean hauled himself up above ground level, took a cursory glance at his surroundings, bent his knees one last time, wrenched his shoulders around, and levered himself out of the well. Even as he rolled behind the stones that surrounded it, he was camouflaged. The rain had turned the ground to liquid mud.

No one saw him. It was daytime, but there was little light; it was smothered beneath the churning clouds of the Season, which coiled and writhed in the sky, plotting some new onslaught. What illumination there was had a smoky yellow quality.

Crouching, Kean clung to the well he had emerged from. It was a small one, set off to one side of the building he had recently vacated. He had a view along the length of the veranda. Standing shin-deep in the mud were scores of men and women who had gathered at the bottom of the old lake outside Dagman's rotting residence.

The largest of the wells was the focal point for the crowd; this was where Hawkerman and Ax stood with Snakebite. The Cruiser was tightly bound from the waist up, and Ax's big hands were on his shoulders, feeling for the smallest twitch of resistance—and ready, also, to shove Snakebite straight into the well at a signal from the team leader. They faced Dagman's two-story mansion, with Cara and Wil and Wailing Joe positioned to watch their backs. Cara and Wil carried gutguns, the favored projectile weapon of the Cruisers—stubby metal crossbows. Kean guessed that they had been taken in a battle with Snakebite's men. Barb and the other twin, Gil, were not in sight, and Hawkerman did not have his own gun with him.

Dagman's Cruiser guard lined the veranda, weapons at the ready, and Cruisers comprised at least half the crowd that had followed Hawkerman here. A team member again, Kean assessed the situation, calculating how he could work to best effect. Not by showing himself, that was for sure.

Hawkerman called to the house, "I'm not waiting much longer. He's going to die."

Kean had a good enough angle on the scene to see Frumitch come out from under the veranda, smiling peaceably. "Hold on there," he called back in his light voice. "The big man's on his way."

There was movement on the veranda again. Dagman's heavy form lumbered out of the house. Behind him came Frumitch, and the cloaked man: Grollat, the Bleacher commander.

FIFTEEN

Dagman's rumbling voice carried easily through the heavy air.

"Why are you causing trouble, Hawkerman? There's only one way it can end."

Hawkerman called back, "Your man killed my brother. I want to know why."

"You don't know that."

"I do." Hawkerman held up a small object. "One of his people took this from Fireface. He wore it on his cloak. We took it back when Snakebite tried to kill me, too, up where the big cats live. I told you your men don't know how to handle themselves in the outlands."

Snakebite shouted, "Let him kill me and then cut them down!"

Dagman smiled, showing his up-reaching tooth. "See what I mean, Hawkerman? You got nothing to trade with. Let my man go, and I'll let your team live—when I've finished with you."

Hawkerman ignored the threat. "I want to know why Snakebite went after my brother."

"What does he say?"

"He says Fireface attacked him. I don't believe him."

"And you want me to agree with you and not him? Trader, get ready to die."

Those in the crowd who were onlookers started to retreat. The Cruisers among them stood their ground.

Hawkerman spread his arms wide. "Dagman. You know the gun I carry?"

"I see you didn't bring it with you. Very wise."

"It's pointing at you now. Along with a bow in the hands of someone who doesn't miss much. You're fat and you're slow, and I reckon between them, my people could get off four shots before you could make it back to your door."

Everyone looked around. On the outskirts of the lake, Barb showed herself at the side of one of the acacias, bow aimed. Only Kean saw Gil, because he knew the kind of place he'd pick in order to make the shot. He was lying on top of one of the Cruiser wagons, much closer in.

"I don't see your gun," Dagman blustered.

"No? Suits me fine. Now you tell me the truth of why my brother had to die."

Dagman hesitated and glanced back at the hooded man. Kean thought he saw the man shake his head without hardly moving it all.

Dagman shouted, "You think I won't take a chance? You think I'm afraid of *you*?"

It was all about to happen. Kean stood up. He made his voice loud and clear.

"Dagman ordered the killing. Because he works for the Bleachers."

A dozen gutguns were trained on him immediately. "Kean?" Wailing Joe said incredulously. "Kean?"

Kean walked in slowly through the mud, coming between the two groups. *Don't get too near Hawkerman; split the enemy fire.*

"The Cruisers do what the Bleachers tell them to, and in return, the Bleachers fill these wells for them." Kean waved his arm at the wells. "It's a deal. Keep the Wanderers in line and get water."

Hawkerman was working out how best to use the situation to his advantage. The crowd began to advance again in curiosity. Someone shouted, "How do you know that?"

Another voice called, "We'd know about it if there was water brought in."

"How?" Kean answered. "How would you know? It comes through an underground water pipe that runs all the way from the Pyramid. I'm telling you, the Cruisers get ten percent of all Bleacher water." *Create division within the enemy ranks:* "And Dagman gets secret gifts on top."

Dagman found his voice, furious. "That's a lie! You're dead, too, boy! This is lies, people! Ask him again—how could he know these things?"

"I've been there," Kean said. "Just now returned. Look at the clothes."

Dagman called to his men, "On my signal, take them all out. I'd rather die than listen to this craziness."

"You don't need to take my word for it," Kean called out to the Wanderers. "The man by Dagman—the one you can't see because of the cloak? He's a Bleacher. He'll take his hood off, and he'll tell you all about it. Ask him to!"

His hood still low over his face, Grollat walked forward to the edge of the veranda. He appeared to glance once at Dagman, and Dagman screamed, "Kill them!" and it all happened.

Grollat drew a short-barreled pacifor from under his cloak and brought it up to point at Kean.

Dagman collapsed on the veranda, shot by Gil.

Cruisers opened fire, and the first to be hit was Snakebite, now a human shield for Hawkerman and Ax. His life was done; he went down the well with hands tied and a gutgun bolt through his chest.

Kean was down and rolling as a ball of blue electricity hissed into the mud beside him.

Hawkerman and those with him were diving for cover behind the rocks around the well while Gil and Barb fired into the densely packed veranda.

Some of the Cruisers were assaulted by men in the crowd and fired back at them instead of Hawkerman's team.

Grollat fired again as a wounded Cruiser blundered into him. The shot went wide, and they both went down. Kean ran at Grollat, butting into the Bleacher hard as he was rising to his knees. Wrestling for the pacifor, Kean found himself aided by Frumitch of all people. Two against one wasn't enough with the Commander; Frumitch took a heavy blow in the mouth, and Kean was hurled back, too. But he had the pacifor. Lying on his back, he set the thing off, his finger finding the trigger and squeezing it before he had aimed the weapon. A Cruiser was blown backward, thudding into the wall. Grollat flung himself through the door of the house and disappeared—and Frumitch was shouting through bleeding lips, "Get the hooded man! Forget the Wanderers—don't let him go!"

He dragged two Cruisers with him and pushed them through the door. They went after Grollat, and Frumitch lay on the boards of the veranda to avoid being shot and screamed, "Stop firing! It's finished! Stop firing!"

He kept on repeating the command. It took a while for the message to reach all parties concerned. Hawkerman had taken Cara's gutgun and used it to good effect. Cruisers were firing back, and Ax and Wailing Joe had been hit. When he sensed the conflict was dying down, Hawkerman shouted to stop firing, too. The violence came to a stop bit by bit, with some shots still being fired into the crowd by the Cruisers farthest from Frumitch. Two of them were overwhelmed by Wanderers as they reloaded. There were a couple last sporadic shots, and then all was quiet.

Frumitch got to his feet. "No more firing!" he shouted unnecessarily.

There was a last burst of action. The Cruisers who had gone after Grollat reappeared. "Get away—get clear! He's set it on fire!"

Kean staggered away from the veranda, still clutching the pacifor.

Smoke drifted out of the house, and then flames were seen. Grollat had overturned the lamp to cover his flight. The wooden building would have burned better if it had not been for the sudden and cataclysmic return of the rain: a solid flood that broke upon the Lakes with such power that men and women were knocked to the ground.

Human disputes were put aside for a while in the struggle against the elements. Kean forced his way to Hawkerman, who was with Cara and Wil by the big well, satisfying himself that the wounds Ax and Wailing Joe had were not life-threatening. Ax had a shallow gash in his side, and Wailing Joe had a bolt embedded in his hip. Otherwise Hawkerman's team was unscathed.

The downpour washed the mud from Kean's Bleacher clothing. Hawkerman saw him, and rain ran into his mouth as he smiled. They bellowed at one another, both smiling.

"So you really were there!" Hawkerman shouted. "What kind of fool are you, Kean?"

"Me, a fool? What about you?"

Gil and Barb joined them, bent low by the rains.

"You all right?" Barb wanted to know of her man.

Ax grunted, "I'll live. Old Joe's found trouble again."

Wailing Joe said from where he lay in the mud, "That's all you know. I'll live a while longer, and don't you think otherwise."

Cara asked Gil, "You killed Dagman?"

Gil, dumb, slapped his hand against his collarbone, and Barb agreed. "He took it in the shoulder."

On the veranda, Frumitch rose from the group of Cruisers gathered close around their fallen leader. He staggered over to the well, at times knocked sideways by the rain, watched all the way by Hawkerman and the others.

The Cruiser lieutenant called out, "You happy now?"

"What do you want?"

Frumitch flopped down in the mud beside Wailing Joe. He looked happy enough himself, not at all troubled by the recent happenings. He lisped, "It's a busy day, Hawkerman."

"Yes. How's Dagman?"

"Died of his wounds just this moment."

Hawkerman studied Frumitch. The little man remained unconcerned under his stare.

"Is that right," Hawkerman said.

"I don't know about right—that's what happened."

Frumitch killed him, Kean thought in disbelief.

Hawkerman said at last, "Well . . . these things happen."

You could feel Frumitch relax. "He wouldn't have wanted to live, any case. He hated failure."

"I asked you, what do you want?"

Frumitch said, "We got to do some talking. Fast."

It was Cara who answered him, vicious in her hatred. "We don't talk to Cruiser killers."

Frumitch ignored her, saying to Hawkerman, "I'll need you and the boy."

"Why?"

"We had a good thing going with the Pyramid. It depended on trust, like all business. Now the trust has gone. So . . ." Frumitch looked at Kean. "Got any ideas about what happens next, boy?"

Kean said, "The man with the hood—he's on his way home. He's coming back with all the force they can raise, and he's going to hit the Lakes. Teach us a lesson to keep us in line. Cruisers as well as Wanderers."

Frumitch nodded, bright-eyed. "Yeah. That's how I see it, too. So we got to talk." He pointed. The crowd had not gotten smaller. If anything, there were more Wanderers here than before, soaked in rain and mud. "Look—all these people. Not just Cruisers. Your people. They need you, Hawkerman."

"And you think talking's going to save them?"

Frumitch stood up with difficulty in the mud and rain. "It depends what we talk about."

Following the fire, the stench of burned wood and skins was enhanced by the dampness in the Cruiser headquarters. They were in the largest room in the building, where arms were stored and the guards slept. The ceiling here was undamaged, and the space was just big enough to accommodate the gathering. Outside the rain still lashed down, striking at the wooden walls in an occasional frenzy, loud.

There were forty of them sitting here on the floor, half of them Cruisers represented by Frumitch, the new head man. Hawkerman and Kean had Cara with them, as well as

Wailing Joe, whose age and wisdom had gained him entry to the meeting. Cara crouched beside him, pressing a pad onto his hip. The bolt had not penetrated far and had come out reasonably cleanly. He hid the pain as well as he could, proud to be there.

Of the other Wanderers, Kean recognized only one, Cancher, the weapons expert who had allied himself with Fireface. It was he who was doing the talking now.

"You want us to fight? Fight for what, Frumitch? So you can go on mistreating us?"

"No. So you live long enough to die a natural death. Which we all might just do if you Wanderers join up with my men. You were going to fight, anyway, for Fireface, so what's the problem?"

When Cancher only gave him a sullen look, Frumitch turned to Hawkerman. "What's your view? If you come in with me, then others will."

Hawkerman was watching Cara at work on old Joe. He said slowly, "I can get my team out of here and turn my back on the whole thing. The question is, do I want to?"

Cara said immediately, "Yes. You do."

One of the Wanderers, a successful trader, said, "We could all leave. Wait for the trouble to die down."

"That would just make the Bleachers' job easier," Frumitch sneered. "They could destroy everything here and pick us off one by one—those of us who had the experience to survive the Season. And besides, Cruisers don't run, friend."

Another Wanderer chipped in. "We've listened to enough from Cruiser scum. I want to hear Hawkerman."

There was a murmur of agreement from the Wanderers. As far as Kean could tell from his expression, the respect and popularity Hawkerman had was more burdensome to him than gratifying.

He addressed Cancher. "Fireface had a plan, right? He wanted to attack the Pyramid, and he was going to do it right in the middle of the Season. Yes?"

"How did you know?"

"That's how I'd have done it. Could you still mount that attack?"

"We might be able to. If you take your brother's place."

"That's crazy," Frumitch said. "We got to *defend* ourselves."

Hawkerman stared at him coldly. "You do what you like. You Cruisers, you broke the rules. Working for the Bleachers. Killing for them."

Wailing Joe tried to sit up a little. "You're letting your feelings do the talking, Hawkerman," he gasped out. "It's not good odds, taking on the Pyramid."

"Joe, in the last hour, everything's changed—or didn't you notice?"

"That's just smart words. We're talking high risk here. The highest."

Cara spoke, showing emotion in a way that was unlike her. "Don't—don't do it, Hawkerman."

"Listen, Frumitch," Hawkerman said, pointing a finger at him. "You sit here and let the Bleachers come to you, and you'll suffer the result: they dictate any terms they want when it comes to your little conspiracy about the water. As in, they don't give you a single drop more. Which affects us all. If you take the fight to them, and you get some success, then they might have to negotiate. It's the only option we have."

"No—it isn't," Cara shouted. "You're not thinking straight—none of this is anything to do with you! You don't get involved—that's how we survive! You said it yourself—we can trail out of here—they'll never find us if you don't want them to!"

"Not today, Cara," was all Hawkerman said.

Kean got to his feet. He'd earned the right to be heard, and yet he felt strange and regretful about it. He had the feeling that to speak at this time would be to finally declare himself a man and let fall the privileges and immunities of youth. Like that wooden knife old Joe had made for him years ago. He'd grown too old for it, and he'd felt sad when he knew he'd never carry it again.

Now people were looking at him, because he was up and not speaking. So he cleared his throat and spoke.

"Fireface wasn't a fool. If he thought he could do some damage with just a few men, then with more of us, and with the Cruisers attacking, too, there must be a chance. If they're not afraid of taking on the Pyramid."

That got an angry response from the Cruisers, and Frumitch had to quiet his men down.

"That's big talk, boy. What we'd have to know is whether Fireface stood a chance, and if we've got the time to beat the Bleachers to it."

"Well," Kean said, feeling bolder, "it takes a good while to get back there, even traveling underground. Then that man has to call one of their meetings, like we're having now. Then he's got to organize his forces. Then most likely he's going to wait for better weather conditions. He won't expect us to come to him."

"So what was the plan?" Hawkerman asked Cancher.

"We had fast wagons made. They're still there. So are the explosives. Gas bombs. I made them in the rocks, months ago. The idea is to sweep through the windmills when the wind is good and high, set the charges against the Pyramid."

Hawkerman smiled. "It's good. Let the weather do the fighting. Blow holes in the Pyramid and let some air in."

"You got to get through the windmills first," Wailing Joe pointed out. Suddenly he did not sound so pessimistic, however.

"We'll have Cruiser support," Hawkerman said casually. "So, you going to make a name for yourself, Frumitch?"

Other Cruisers answered for him.

"Yes."

"Do it!"

"You're going to get yourselves killed," Cara whispered to Hawkerman. "Please."

Hawkerman just shook his head at her. "Plans, Frumitch—let's get on with it."

Frumitch did not like his authority being usurped. "First things first. You're talking about some fast wagons. Well, I never yet saw a wagon could travel rapid through a foot and a half of slopping mud."

"You will," said Cancher.

SIXTEEN

The warlike Cruisers had accepted the call to arms with fierce joy. With the exception of Cancher, every one of the Wanderers had been tasked to enlist fighters from the more peaceable Lakesiders.

Frumitch had been shown the wagons that could do the impossible. They were of a size where, when it had been vital, they could be hidden from Cruiser eyes in small tents, and they had a unique design: tiny rounded tubs of aluminum set not on wheels but on short wide skis. There were no engines; the five vehicles were wind-powered, using sails. At the stern of each was a pole which could be levered into the mud to alter direction.

Cancher explained, "Each takes two men, one to fight and one to steer. The crew has to be small and light. This is the time when you get all the winds blowing right to the Pyramid and the White beyond. You just got to aim them straight. Last Season we practiced. These things skid over a wet surface faster than you would believe. A little unpredictable, which is why we built five of them, to get through the windmills. The plan was, some men start a diversion on the east side of the Pyramid, and then these race in from the north. Set the charges and hope to live long enough to see a couple of teams arriving to escort them out again. The wind does the rest, if it blows strong enough."

Fireface had planned to withdraw and strike again often. Any success would bring him support in the Lakes.

Hawkerman said, "The first time is the best. They only got simple weapons in the windmills—bows and such. The wagons wouldn't be hit much if we move fast enough. After that, they'd have the fields better protected. We should go for one decisive strike. Nothing wrong with the plan, only we make it bigger. Make it a major diversion—at least half the force we raise, Cruisers and Wanderers together. As well as that, send a party along through this water pipe, too—split Bleacher attention all we can, so we can make the charges count. The final band follows the attack wagons to go through any holes we make."

No one raised objections to the tactics he outlined. There was one problem, however: the bomb team had lost two men. One had died under torture by Dagman, and the other had been the young man who had been so foolhardy at the Face-Off.

"Kean and me. We're light enough," Hawkerman said. "All right with you, Kean?"

"Oh—yes." There was no other answer he could make, and no other answer he wanted to make.

∽

The sky was dense and murky if you had the willpower to look upward to see it through the gale-force winds that blew the rain near horizontally. Kean was battered and bruised by the lances of water, protected only by the Bleacher clothes he still wore because he had the notion the disguise could be useful if he gained entry to the city.

The call to arms had raised over two hundred Wanderers in a few hours, both men and women. Less in number, the Cruisers were far better equipped, although Hawkerman had his pump gun once more, and Kean had the short pacifor, which might or might not have plenty of shots left in it.

The army of allies came together around the wells, group by group struggling through the mud. When at last they were assembled, their number at least was impressive.

The rapid strike force was sorted out quickly. Since Kean and Hawkerman had no experience with the ski wagons, they were assigned to different drivers. Kean's partner would be Cancher himself. Fifty of the fittest Cruisers were picked to be the contingent that would penetrate the city and do what damage they could when—if—the walls were breached. Their first duty would be to drag the attack vehicles into place outside the perimeter of the Pyramid.

Thereafter, the process of dividing the forces slowed considerably. Voices grew hoarse under the torrent of rain-water as bands of men and women shuffled this way and that, directed to one of the other two brigades: the diversionary force and the detachment that would travel underground through the water conduit. The Wanderers were unused to discipline of any kind, and it was only the threat of a Bleacher onslaught that kept the whole business from disintegrating into a succession of noisy arguments.

The party of underground invaders filed into the wooden residence, previously Dagman's, where they climbed down into the water tunnel. It was a conjuring trick, the way so many went in and the house never filled up. Ax was their leader. Barb was going with the diversionary band, out in the open where her arrows would be of more use.

She said to her man, standing on the porch and waving his men through into the house, "Don't be too brave. They'd have that entrance well defended all year round."

He grinned savagely. "About time they got a scare, then. But we'll fall back if we have to."

Frumitch was talking to Hawkerman. "Last chance to make any adjustments, if you've thought of any."

"Make it look real—that's all I ask. Take their attention. Stick to the plan."

Frumitch nodded briskly and walked away to lead the diversionary group out from the Lakes. In order to come in from an unexpected direction and thus make it look like a well-thought-out assault, they had the farthest to travel.

The attack wagons themselves had to take a circuitous route to get into place for the run at the Pyramid. By now it was possible a force of Pacifiers could be setting out from the Pyramid on a punitive expedition.

And the wind blew and blew. Frumitch and his little army were hurried toward their fate by its urgency, stumbling across the mud in a shambling welter of leather-clad bodies fighting to keep themselves from bumping together and bringing each other down. It was not a sight to strike fear into an enemy.

"Anything to say to the men?" Cancher shouted at Hawkerman.

"What's to say? No one could hear me, anyway."

Hawkerman waved an arm, and his band followed him out of the Lakes with no more grace and elegance than Frumitch's men had shown. The shining little wagons looked impossibly delicate.

Those left behind took shelter and prayed the Bleachers would not come.

∽

"What's going on?" Essa had called across the cavern to the guard outside the Self-Examination Cells.

"You don't need to know. You're not part of Arcone anymore," he shouted back.

There were at least a hundred Pacifiers arrayed around the basin in squads of ten. This could not be normal. Now nine more men had come up to one of the detention caves, bringing a uniform with them. Until that time Essa, had not even been aware it was occupied; then one of the soldiers went in and brought out a brute of a man, seemingly about as wide as he was tall, whose long matted hair testified to him spending many weeks in contemplation of his faults.

Truly she was now a nonperson: the man stripped naked to put on the uniform, laughing and joking with the others as if she were not there at all. If she had not guessed why he was being freed, she would have known when he flexed his stupendous biceps and grinned.

Later, her guard's turn of duty finished, and he was replaced by another Pacifier, who brought more food to Essa. The man reeled in the cage in order to pass her the square tray. On it was a water beaker, another portion of artificial protein, and a small box.

The man was short, clean, and efficient, and he had a grievance. "Thanks to you, I miss the peak moment of my career."

Crouched on the steel bars, Essa was looking in the box. It contained three small pills. The guard was still grousing. "You train and rehearse for an attack, year in and year out, and then they give you guard duty on the one day you could use your hard-won skills."

The pills were not of a common type. She asked, "What are these?"

"With the Commander's compliments. Take them with the last meal you have, and by the time we do the business, you won't feel a thing. They'll make you happy. Sleepy. It's a favor from the Commander."

"I don't want them."

"You will. And it'll only be you, me, and the Commander who'll know it isn't blind courage you're showing when the big drop begins. Take 'em. He must think a lot of you. It's not supposed to be like this."

Essa hesitated.

"Keep them by you—that's what I'd do."

It was hard to refuse an offer kindly meant. "I'll keep them. But I won't take them."

"I would."

"And my last meal will be . . . ?"

"First thing tomorrow. Since you ask."

"Good. I mean—I did want to know."

He began to reel her back to her isolation.

"Wait!" she cried.

He paused with sullen patience. As she swayed inside the cage, Essa thought, *I must be so terrified I don't even take things in anymore.* What she said was, "You mentioned— you said something about an attack. Are the outlanders attacking, then?"

"Don't be foolish. We're attacking them. Going to remind them who's who around here."

"Oh."

"And I'm going to miss it." His sense of ill-usage returned, souring him. "You thought your friends might be coming, did you? Coming to get you?"

It was exactly the hope that had flitted across her mind. "No, I—"

"They wouldn't, and they couldn't, and even if they did, why d'you think I'm here? To serve you food and wipe your face afterward? No, I'm here so that if you try anything—or anyone else does on your behalf—I can execute justice then and there. Like this."

He worked a lever on the block-and-tackle mechanism, and the cage dropped a few feet. Essa fell onto the hard metal bars, clutching the tray. She felt the cage rising up again and her heart pounding against it.

"Still got them?" the Pacifier called. "Don't drop them now!" He laughed.

෴

It seemed to Kean the initial journey took very little time. In the swirling darkness, blasted by the winds, one moment ran into the next and was lost in a dark medley of identical moments while he hauled at the wagon and tried to get it to slide in a straight course over the mud. Getting the wagon to move was encouragingly easy; getting it to go where you wanted it to was another matter entirely with the gale beating at your back, and your feet slipping at every step. Up ahead, Hawkerman was their guide, a vague shape that might have been part of the tempest itself; behind them, forty Cruisers slopped along, grousing about their wet feet.

It could be worse. It *would* be worse at some point in the Season.

The shape that was Hawkerman came to a stop and extended itself. He was holding up a hand. The attack team leaned back into the wind to be still, and abruptly Kean lost his footing and found himself lying on his back in the mud.

Hawkerman came back to them. "We're there," he bellowed. "Get up, Kean."

Kean rose muddily to his feet, helped by Cancher, who called, "What is it?"

"We're there," Hawkerman shouted.

"How can you tell?"

"Lights."

The rest of the Cruisers struggled up to them, and they all stared into the wet, rolling night. There was a barely defined glow of light visible, although at what distance, it was impossible to calculate.

∾

She was tempted. The apprehension was growing in her, and she felt close to tears all the time. Now she wished she didn't know when the awful event would be staged. Wouldn't it be better to take the drug and float away from the fear? Except that then she would not be herself, she would be a stranger who smiled vacantly as the waters took her under. It was all she had wanted, to be herself, not a creature of Arcone, an automaton. Suddenly, an idea came to her—another use for the pills. Just maybe, if her warder was drugged, there'd be a chance of getting away. It wasn't much of a chance, but it was something she could *do*.

The guard was not watching her. He had gone halfway down the steps to talk to one of his compatriots. They were listening to a sound Essa could hear, too: the rolling of heavy wheels, a whine of electricity coming from somewhere close to the cavern.

The only way to break up a pill safely was to bite it. It was bitter, and she was quick to take the crumbled pieces from her mouth and begin the task of disguising them in the portion of protein. Make it look as though she had eaten at least some of the food, and then it wouldn't matter too much if it didn't look perfect. If only the first guard was still with her. He'd gobble it up all right. While she was engaged in doing something, she felt better. Disguising the pills was a work of art, in its way—if, probably, her last.

She felt better still when the man ate the scraps. He did it without enjoyment—it was something to do while his mind was elsewhere. Things of great import were going on, and no news was reaching him.

The medication he had ingested had no effect on him at all.

⁓

The waiting was long. With no communication with the other groups, it was hard to keep faith in the plan that had been so swiftly conceived at the Lakes. Frumitch's team might have lost their bearings, might have been subject to attack from a Bleacher party, and without the diversion, the little strike force stood no chance.

All along Hawkerman had said they would know when to make the run. They did.

Despite the buffeting of the wind, Kean was beginning to doze, keeling over in the mud, when the night sky began to light up around the Pyramid in a spectacular way. The diversionary force had arrived, attacking the windmills just as the armed might of Arcone streamed out from the main gate. First there were sparks of light and the sounds of shouting men off to the right—much closer than Kean had thought possible—and almost at the same moment, the great gates of the city lifted, and a highway of light swept down the fields, picking out the marauders among the windmills. Emerging from the Pyramid came long, tubular troop carriers, with belt tracks turned by their many wheels.

"Time to go! Haul up the sails!" Hawkerman called out.

The next minute Kean and Cancher were scudding along like two boys lying face-to-face in a bathtub. In the stern, Cancher reclined on his back wrestling with the sail lines, which had already scored raw passages in his hands. Bracing himself against the sides of the flimsy metal vehicle, Kean sat in the front. From there he was able to see the first casualty. The wagons were racing along in an uneven wedge formation, Kean and Cancher leading. The tub nearest theirs bounced into the whirling air and somersaulted. It had hit a rock exposed by the tearing winds. The high-speed motion of its demise made Kean gag with horror. It was lost in the darkness before he could blink. Maybe the Cruisers following on foot would pick up the team on their way to support the strike force.

There were eerie moments of quiet as the wind shifted. The roaring in his ears would stop, and he would hear the cries of fighting men. Then the sail would billow with a *crack*, and the ski wagon would accelerate, sliding left or right till Cancher had it aligned again. You didn't steer these things: you aimed them.

Kean had not thought to ask how they would navigate the ditch that marked the limits of Arcone, and was startled when their sheer speed shot them straight over it into the wind-battered corn stubble. A glance behind and he saw another of the wagons slewing sharply into the ditch, one of its skis flying free. He gripped the pacifor and squirmed around to face front.

At once there was a dark mass to his left—the first of the windmills. Their superstrong vanes were spinning angrily, and slits at the top showered down light—and arrows. Over to the right, the fighting raged between the Wanderers and the Bleachers, a bloody bedlam more like a riot than a battle. The Bleacher transport vehicles had ground to a halt, surrounded by struggling men and women, and Pacifiers were streaming from the Pyramid to join the fray.

SEVENTEEN

With no clear target to aim at, there didn't seem any point in firing the pacifor. Cancher was trying to navigate between the windmills, and the corn stubble was slowing them considerably. Behind them another wagon was gone, Hawkerman's tub; it had lost the wind and skidded to a halt. It was quickly surrounded by field workers from the adjacent windmill.

They carried long scythes.

The winds strengthened in one of those hurricane squalls so typical of the time of year. Their ski wagon shot forward at a vastly increased rate. Then the darkened corner of the Pyramid was looming up in front of them. Cancher leaned back and hauled, and the wagon spun out of control. From behind them, there was a white-hot explosion, followed swiftly by an even greater and brighter detonation. Suddenly another shape careened out of the darkness and rammed them: the other surviving attack wagon. Kean hit his face on the aluminum of his own wagon and tasted blood. The next thing he knew, Cancher was wrestling him out of the overturned tub.

"The bombs—where?" Cancher was screaming, wild with adrenaline in the tempestuous winds.

They scrabbled in the mud under the wagon. Cancher bent his back and lifted it, and Kean had his hand on one of the bombs, a solid mass of leather and metal. There was a tag on it, which you had to tear off to let air mix with a chemical compound. Cancher snatched the bomb from Kean and was ripping at the tag even as he staggered to the sloping wall of the Pyramid.

"No—no!" Kean bawled, his hand already on the second of the two explosive devices. They had to be detonated at the same time, to be sure of penetrative effect.

The two men from the other team were mauled by the wind as they prepared their own charges and careered toward the Pyramid. Another white explosion, and when Kean looked around, Cancher had vanished, and the wall still stood, undamaged. One of the members of the other team was down, lying still, while his companion was kneeling, with his hands holding his belly as if he were trying to make sure that nothing spilled out.

A ghost shrieked, "Take them, Kean—behind me!"

Hawkerman was being blown toward him, a reeling figure spattered with mud and blood, and pursued by a score of field workers, whose long weapons were uncontrollable in the hurricane-force winds. There was no sign of the

Cruisers who were supposed to charge in when the walls were pierced.

Kean fired the pacifor. The bolt cut a bending blue streak through the violent air, skewed by the onrushing gale, and passed over the heads of the men with their scythes. The use of a Bleacher weapon confused them. They fell back.

Hawkerman had gathered the two bombs from the Wanderers who had fallen near Cancher and was blundering to the Pyramid. The field workers started forward once more. Kean fired again, and again they fell back.

When Kean turned to the city wall, Hawkerman was already struggling back toward him in slow motion, empty-handed, making dream-like progress against the windstorm. Kean snatched up the last bomb and hurled it high, letting the winds take it toward the Pyramid. The action threw him forward on the wind, and then in a starburst of light, he was slammed back again by a final tremendous triple explosion, which punched him to the ground with such a thrust that he imagined his back had been broken.

The bomb he had thrown so helplessly had been detonated by the others set by Hawkerman. Kean could not see what effect they had had. His eyesight was blurred, and he had bitten his tongue. He tasted blood. Dazed, he fumbled for the pacifor in the mud and tried to stand upright. The wind carried him like a scrap of cloth, bundling him toward the Pyramid. Hawkerman was crouched, waiting for him.

"What now?" Kean called as Hawkerman gripped his arm.

"Only one way to go!" the older man screamed back.

They let the wind take them and rush them toward a dark ragged perforation that had appeared in the Pyramid's hitherto impervious walls.

Mighty Arcone was breached.

They were carried into a chamber which held giant grain silos. The gloom was not total; the ceiling was lined with phosphor strips. Two Bleachers lay dead against the far wall, where they had been thrown by the explosion. In here the wind sounded like a wild beast in pain as it howled around them.

"Not enough damage!" Hawkerman shouted in despair, unhitching his compressed-air gun from his back. Kean grabbed him and pulled him to the far wall. Taking out his knife, he stabbed at the wall; the knife slid downward and slit it open like the belly of a greenback. They tumbled into a second chamber with the wind as their eager companion. This was a distribution area for the grain, with a profusion of carts, tubs, and scales.

"See how it's done?" Kean shouted. "It's easy!"

Hawkerman raised his gun and fired. Behind Kean, a Pacifier fell dead in an open doorway with a steel dart through his chest. It was Hawkerman saving him from the charjaws all over again. This time he felt the shock of seeing sudden, violent human death.

Now Hawkerman yelled, "You'll be safer without me!"

It took Kean a moment to comprehend what he meant. Dirty though he was, his appearance was still that of a Bleacher.

"What about the Cruisers?" he yelled back.

"They'll be here! Go! Do what you can!"

In another instant Kean understood what he needed to do. He ran to the doorway, feeling footsteps thumping along somewhere above him. Voices were calling. He turned back. Hawkerman was already stabbing at an inner wall with savage concentration, and the farther the wind entered, the more it grew in intensity. The torn material of the plastic wall flapped with a hysterical rippling sound. Kean forced his way back across the chamber. Grain containers were rolling everywhere, propelled by the wind. He caught hold of a barrel-size tub and dragged it to Hawkerman.

"Get in. Wait!" he called fiercely.

He could see that Hawkerman did not like the idea of hiding, and added at the top of his voice, "It's the wise move!"

As Hawkerman began to lower himself into the container, Kean sprinted back to the doorway he'd come from, and the winds shoved him headlong into a wide corridor. Led by a single Pacifier, a band of citizens was running toward him.

∽

Essa had felt the force of the explosion when it came. The chain holding the cage trembled, and the vibration continued in the metal bars for some seconds.

It did not cause much commotion in the big reservoir, since it was by now all but empty of human life. The assembled Pacifiers had been joined by another force and, ducking their heads as they passed through it, had marched away through a low portal that led underground—to the world outside, she suspected. It seemed that the Pyramid was indeed under attack. The dismal atmosphere of the cavern had been enlivened by a charge of manic excitement; soon her guard had been met by some others, and together they had ushered the rest of the prisoners down from the cells and out of the reservoir.

Essa watched and let hope grow larger within her.

If it was a battle, it was going badly for the Arconians. A small contingent of battered Pacifiers returned through the underground tunnel and left at once by the doors that led up into the main structure of the Pyramid. Within a minute, some of them were back in the reservoir, swept along in the rapid arrival of the Prime Conscience, accompanied by an elite guard made up of the largest Pacifiers. Among them were the giant who had been the first prisoner to be freed, and her own personal guard. Way beneath her, Maxamar issued orders.

Some of his men reentered the tunnel. Now Maxamar gazed up at Essa in the cage and spoke to the guard. It was too far away to have any idea of what he was saying, but in her condition of readiness, Essa knew, with perfect clarity, that the moment had come. Maxamar had killed her parents, and now he would kill her.

Slowly her guard began to ascend the rocky steps. It seemed to take a lot out of him. Were the drugs at last having some effect?

∽

Kean did not have to act scared; he *was* scared as, pretending to be a resident of Arcone, he babbled to its citizens and the Pacifier about the devastating explosion. His six-fingered hand he held hidden in the other as, for good measure, he added the lie that he had seen fighting in the fields just beyond the gaping rent in the outer wall. It was the kind of panic situation the group had expected, and he was immediately forgotten as they argued about how best to seal off the grain chambers. A human wall was, he had time to gather, an unpopular option.

He ran on, his purpose set in his mind. He would see what he could do for the girl. Finding her was not the only problem. Any Arconians who were not already fighting were preparing to do so, setting up barricades of beds and household furniture, either outside the many individual doors or across the corridors themselves. At every such obstacle, he was asked for news; the confusion was total. Children cried and were comforted too urgently by their mothers. A young boy of about ten was looking for his parents. For his safety, Kean directed him to the last barricade he had passed—and confessed to being lost himself, on his way to the reservoir. With simple innocence, the boy gave him the directions he needed.

∽

An ominous groaning noise echoed around the reservoir as the guard made his way up the uneven stairway. Between her feet, Essa could see the water eddying, moving as if disturbed. Her guard came on, quite obviously not as clear-headed or quick as he wished to be. Once he paused to shake his head. It was a creeping nightmare watching him get ever nearer, laborious step by laborious step. The other man remained below on the bottom step; some kind of security. Otherwise the reservoir was deserted until a figure arrived through the main doors, a fast-moving person in a filthy tunic. A messenger, she supposed. Hope had died. She watched dully. Her guard was halfway up the stairs. The dirty civilian Arconian had come to the big Pacifier.

Far beneath her, Kean said, "I must pass!"

"No one passes!" the warrior snarled, suspicious. He was lifting his pacifor.

Kean brought up his own shorter weapon and shot the man in the foot. The blue bolt was weak: the pacifor's reserves were drained. Nevertheless, it had the effect of breaking a bone or two. The man howled and hopped, and Kean smashed the barrel of the gun against his adversary's arm, causing him to drop his electric weapon, which bounced once on a stone step and spiraled down into the reservoir. Kean bashed at the man again, and then went after the other man at a run.

Essa saw the young man pause to fire the short-barreled pacifor again, aiming at the guard above him. The gun emitted no more than a faint blue light, and the young man dropped it and chased after the guard. It couldn't be . . . could it? She saw his pale hair. She still wouldn't let herself believe it. He was gaining on the half-doped guard. It *was* him.

Lower down, the huge Pacifier yelled out a warning, limping up the stairway. The guard turned, and his astonishment at seeing his pursuer revived him. He scrambled up the last steps any old way, like a drunk in a hurry.

Kean was leaping up the stairs as fast as he could, but the guard was there before him, fumbling with the workings of the block and tackle. Essa felt the cage lurch. With no time for ceremony, the guard disengaged the chain completely, and in an instant, Essa was falling, banging from bar to bar as the cage dropped toward the swirling water. There was not a thought in her mind, only a tumult of horror.

The cage did not so much fall into the water as collide with it. Then its weight took it down, and the water was all there was.

Kean saw the water engulf the cage and drag it under. In a fury, he charged the guard into the nearest Self-Examination Cell. There was a jangle as they fell in a heap. Keys. Kean wrenched them from the man's belt and staggered back to the steps. The giant was nearly on top of them, his face distorted with pain and hatred.

For one frozen moment, Kean hesitated. The first guard arrived behind him and grabbed him, trapping both his arms against his chest. Kean bent his legs and twisted and shoved. Locked together, they staggered back to the cells, where Kean smashed the man against solid rock, breaking his hold. He got a grip on him, spun around and heaved, and the guard found himself thrown into the arms of the oncoming colossus. They went down the stairway backward, bumping and crashing against stone and rock.

For Kean, it was four light, quick steps to the big drop, and he jumped as far as he could, out and up . . . and far, far down to the water.

Plummeting through an uprush of air, he saw how disturbed the water was; it had somehow gone into motion. Even if he had been able to swim, it was now charging along so strongly that he would have had no chance of guiding himself. He smacked into the surface of the water as if it were near solid, and then it was like being swallowed by the biggest, hungriest lizard that ever lived.

Everything was traveling the same way, in a roaring, rolling mass. Within seconds, he had arrived at the same place as the cage. The bars battered at him, and he clutched onto them to stop the water from sucking him away. Empty of air, it felt as if his chest would implode. He could not open the cage; it was all he could do to hang onto it, while behind the bars, the girl was drowning.

He had his eyes squeezed shut, and it was a shock when his head was suddenly clear of the water and he could breathe again. He took in deep gulps of air and gazed around wildly as his eyes blinked away the water. Maxamar was flooding the tunnel as a last desperate measure to clear it of the invaders. The reservoir had emptied itself almost completely, except where its floor was lower than the conduit into the tunnel, and this was the case here. There was still six feet of water left, and it was in this shallow pool that the girl lay within the locked cage, submerged, still drowning, if she was not already dead. The keys—where were they? He'd lost them. She was dead. He had to try to get a hand to her and lift her head up . . .

When he moved, painfully, he felt something hard against his stomach: the keys had fallen into his tunic and lodged there. There was a chance, still. He climbed up onto the cage, looking at her body just under the water, a limp bundle. The lock was on the top side of the cage where it had come to rest. The second key he tried fitted and turned the lock easily. He swung the door up, and jumped down and manhandled the body out of the water. Wet and lifeless, she weighed as much as Ax, it seemed, and he lurched to the side of the cage holding her in his arms. They banged hard against the bars—and the girl began to cough up water in short gouts. He felt the spasms going through and through her, felt her trembling, and held on to her.

From over his shoulder, she said faintly, "You can let go now."

EIGHTEEN

He moved her away to arm's length. Couldn't let go, or she'd fall. She was a mess. And she said, "What are you looking at?"

He smiled, and the achievement of not letting her die energized him to the point of elation. "You're okay!"

She took his hands off her shoulders and said, with difficulty since she hadn't yet gotten enough air to talk—and with annoyance that she sounded rather curt and formal—"Yes. You're okay, too. We're both okay."

Then neither of them could think of anything to say, so Kean went back to doing things, because that was what he was good at. He pulled himself out of the cage and reached down for her hand. She took it and, remembering her manners, looked at him full-on and said, "Thank you." Later she was annoyed about that, too, because out of nowhere, a lot of feeling had gone into it. Too much.

When they were out of the water and standing together at the bottom of the reservoir, bruised and numb, angry shouts drew their attention. At this angle, they could see the top of the steps up to the cells. The figure of Maxamar appeared there, by himself, backing up the stairs for some reason that was not yet apparent.

Into view came the first of the Cruisers. They were going up the steps after him, metal adornments glinting, carrying gutguns. Hawkerman was with them.

They heard Maxamar cry out in a rich voice, "In killing me, you kill all that is fine! I despise you!"

One of the Cruisers fired.

Kean and Essa watched. The stubby bolt embedded itself in Maxamar just above the knee. He gasped, and then there was silence.

No more shots were fired; the Cruisers waited, perhaps held back by the enormity of butchering a Prime Conscience.

Maxamar came down one step. "You . . . creatures of dirt!" he choked oddly. The wounded leg gave way, and he staggered, flailing his arms. His long fall was graceful for a whole two seconds, until he cannoned into the rocky walls of the reservoir and became a sack of loose clothes and limbs, plummeting to destruction.

Essa looked at the thing that had been Maxamar, lying on the bottom of the empty reservoir, embracing the slimy rock with wide-stretched arms. Kean pulled her away.

"We're not safe," he told her. "Stay down." He scrambled up the tall steps and appeared at ground level in view of the invaders. He called to Hawkerman and narrowly missed death at the hands of two of the Cruisers, who wanted to shoot him because of the tunic he wore.

⌒

The Cruiser commando force had arrived and entered the torn Pyramid as planned, if a little late. Led by Hawkerman, they stormed through the corridors and passages to the main gates and opened them. While suffering great losses, men and women from the Wanderer army had driven their way through the Bleachers in the fields and now poured into the city, battling their way through the many barricades. Their determination was strengthened when the word passed around that their underground force had been decimated by the flooding ordered by Maxamar.

There was something Essa wanted to do. Had to do. However shaken she had been by her experiences in the reservoir, she would not be swayed. It was what her dead parents would have wished her to do. It was her duty.

Kean told her, "We're not dressed right to be safe. If your people don't try to kill us, then mine will."

"If Arcone is going to be destroyed, I want to be the first to reach the Archive. Everything that's known about our lives here is in that chamber. Do you think it's going to survive intact?"

"I'm more worried about us surviving intact. Why is it so important to you?"

"Don't you ever wonder why we're here? What we're for? Where we came from?"

"We're here to survive," Kean said. "The rest is just words." But his curiosity was stirred. "Come on, then."

It was worse than before in the city. There was no pattern to the fighting, and danger threatened at each corner they turned. Everywhere the Cruisers and Wanderers went, they left holes in the fabric of Arcone. The tearing winds swept through the corridors and apartments, wreaking more damage than the outlanders could ever hope to accomplish by themselves.

After leaving the reservoir, Essa and Kean found themselves almost engulfed in a hand-to-hand struggle between Wanderers and a group of desperate citizens. Kean pulled Essa back, and they took a turning into an empty passageway where a tremendous blast of wind blew them off their feet. They crawled on to the next turning underneath the force of the charging air.

Two minutes later, they stood outside Grollat's apartment, having survived an encounter with a dozen terrified electricians who had gone berserk with fear and were stampeding along like greenback deer, going nowhere but going there very fast.

"Get in," Essa said. It was the pulley-drawn lift, unmanned now. Together they hauled it up through the levels, catching glimpses of carnage as they went.

When they arrived at the level of the Archive, Grollat was waiting for them.

The Commander slid into view as they hauled on the ropes, first his legs and then the rest of him. He was a fearsome sight, alone and with a long gash down his face, yet of all the people they had seen, he looked the least concerned. In one hand he carried one of the short pacifors; the other held a heavy metal bar for action at close quarters. He lifted it.

"Get out," he said evenly.

They did so, slowly. Essa had no doubt he would kill them then and there. Instead he went past them and got into the lift.

He remarked conversationally, "I guess you're going to the Archive."

Essa nodded.

"Stubborn. There's nothing there of any value." He waved the iron bar in a dismissive gesture. "There's nothing anywhere here of any value."

He nodded at Kean with a savage, dangerous smile, his eyes very bright, and let his weapons fall to the floor of the lift. He bent to pull upward on the chains, and the lift started down. The last they saw of the Commander were his burning eyes gazing up at them, communicating some sort of bitter joke.

This level was deserted, and the air was momentarily calm. They pounded along, tired. An eager breeze sprang up from nowhere and overtook them, as if it were on some form of secret scouting mission. Had they known it, this was a warning.

Essa had no lucid idea anymore of what it was she was trying to do. The encounter with Grollat had disoriented her.

The Archive doors were locked. They cut their way in at the corner where Grollat had caught Essa on the last occasion she had attempted to enter the forbidden chamber.

It was tall and stately, a kind of cathedral with holy relics in it. Scores of tiny lights glimmered in the arched ceiling like stars, disseminating a shadowy, hushed atmosphere. At the back of the chamber was the largest and oldest of all the tapestries in Arcone. It was so faded that its original beauty could only be guessed at, and it presented to the beholder an impossibly perfect vision of Arconian life, in which happy, golden-haired children played outside the glorious Pyramid, which was decorated with twining creepers and flowers.

Tall cases lined the walls. As Essa knew, in these were the official histories, perfectly presented, beautifully illustrated, and ultimately no more than propaganda. They held no interest for her. Nor did the oblong cases set on low wooden platforms in a perfect circle, each covered in its own individual tapestry. They held historical artifacts. In the middle of them was a stone box, placed simply on the floor.

Outside in the fields, the fighting had stopped for a while—the winds had reached a new force, flattening the combatants to the ground.

In the Archive, the floor began to tremble. Somewhere in the terminally damaged Pyramid, the hurricane searched its way into a design fault and achieved diabolical velocity. A panel in the flooring shot up and smashed into the ceiling, shattering some of the lights.

"We've got to get out!" Kean shouted.

"Not yet!"

Suddenly the winds were raging in the chamber. Essa fought her way through to the very center of the Archive and wrestled with the lid of the stone box. Behind her, the cabinets against the walls swayed and crashed to the floor. Another floor panel shot up and spun into the outer wall, high up, punching a small hole, a peephole out into the valley. The winds began to work on it.

Kean was at Essa's side. Plastic papers and heavier tablets were flying through the air and ricocheting off the walls. When they had wrested off the top of the box, a soft glow met their eyes. It came from a dehumidifier that preserved the contents of the box—a pile of brittle papers—real paper, the first time Essa had seen such a substance. The sight did not last long. Freed after centuries of captivity, the papers stirred and were snatched into the turbulent air. Essa grabbed at one as it flew up, and held on. She and Kean rose to their feet, reaching for the papers, and then rose higher, caught by a tempest which took hold of them and hurled them up against the big tapestry. All the breath was knocked out of them, and then they were smothered in the dusty tapestry itself as it detached from the wall.

Struggling against asphyxiation, neither Kean nor Essa knew that the outer wall was breaking up into its constituent panels and flying into the night. The winds had decided to make their greatest vortex here in the place most revered by Arconians, to pluck up everything in the room and cast it out into the darkness. The tapestry, with Kean and Essa trapped inside, flew the farthest and highest, an ill-wrapped shroud.

Outside the Pyramid, a few of the adversaries were trying to fight again in the fields, wrestling as much against the terrible wind as against each other, their murderous intent made comical by the conditions. Most lay prone on the ground, where the wind was weakest. Some had their heads raised to the speeding air, and were witnesses as portions of Arcone exploded upward. The electrical system had gone wrong, and the fresh supply of power from the windmills was overloading the regulators. There were eerie flashes of blue light and fizzing sparks. Among the detritus showering out of the Pyramid were many airborne bodies, both the newly dead and those who would die when they hit the ground. It was only when the roof of the garden floor cracked and broke that the annihilation stopped, and the winds traveled unhindered through the great Pyramid, with no more resistance to excite their anger.

Two miles away, the tapestry unfurled as it fell into the fine-grained sand of the Big White with such a bone-crushing thud that Kean and Essa lost consciousness. The Season reminded itself of its duties and let loose a barrage of rain so light that, accelerated by the tempest, it was an instrument of torture, a liquid whip made up of a million lashes.

Essa was the first to come around, with the sharp needles of water stinging her exposed face. The piece of paper from the Archive was still in her hands, and she did not know it.

She shut her eyes so tightly against the painful rain that warm patches of color sprang up behind her eyelids. She allowed herself to believe it: she was alive, and it was so good. *The paper!* She had it. It was getting wet, except the water ran right off, because it was protected by a film of synthetic polymers. *Even so, take no risk with it*. She made herself into a ball and used her whole body to protect it.

∾

Kean groggily assessed their situation and decided that, however long it took, they had to get back to the Lakes by making a wide circuit around the Pyramid, in order to avoid any bloodshed that might still be taking place. As they would discover later, sporadic killing would continue for a good few days.

The sandy terrain was strangely hard underfoot, like walking on densely packed powdered crystal. Even after they had climbed through the crumbling dangers of the low valley walls to the north of the Pyramid, at the mouth of the Big White, the journey took many hours, heads bent low against the wind and rain. Often they fell, and always Essa had the welfare of the precious piece of paper as her priority.

They were not the only stragglers traveling back to the Lakes that afternoon. To avoid being spotted and killed as Bleachers, Kean ensured they kept out of sight of everyone. When a portion of the victorious Wanderer army made a triumphant return into the Lakes, they took advantage of the distraction and crept into the immense hollow from another direction as daylight faded.

It was their great good fortune that one of the first people they came upon was Wailing Joe. He was just about mobile, with a limp that would in time become worse, not better. He took them back to Hawkerman's old camp by the big acacia, where he'd dug himself a covered dwelling to see out the winds. It was amazing he had mustered the strength to do that much. And amazing he could think of so many questions to ask.

"Yes—yes, I'll tell you all about it," Kean said wearily. Instead, when all three were wedged into Joe's bachelor loading, steaming and so tightly packed that it was like being back inside the tapestry, he fell asleep before he was halfway through his story. Beside him, Essa had succumbed to exhaustion long before.

$\backsim$

Ax was dead. Swept to his death in the water tunnel. Of the twins, only Wil was left. His brother was another who was with the horses.

Hawkerman had gone off again almost at once, taking Barb, Wil, and Cara with him, and Kean was left as company for Essa and Wailing Joe. When the remainder of the team reappeared, they were dragging with them the old trailer, a casualty of the Season. Repairs to it took several days.

"This is history being made here," Wailing Joe exclaimed, "and all you've got on your mind is an old trailer."

"It's a good one," Hawkerman replied. "Wouldn't want to lose it."

Over the next two weeks, settled at the Lakes in some degree of comfort now, the team and Essa kept themselves apart from the making of history.

Kean and Essa had time to talk. They were so easy together that both felt it odd that they did not know more about each other. He told her what life was like in a good team. Essa told him about her talks with Grollat, and how her parents had died. About the strictures of life in the Pyramid.

She said, "Things are going to change. Arcone can't go on as it did."

"Maybe you're right. But I don't care anymore. I lost interest in it when it was beaten."

He was so strange, she thought. And so likeable. That hand of his was only a distinguishing mark, that was all. She liked him more because of it, not less.

NINETEEN

awkerman was asked to represent the Wanderers in the formal peace talks, along with Frumitch, and declined, to everyone's surprise. He said privately, "What does a do-gooder get? Abuse. Anyway, give it ten years and we'll be back where we were. The Pyramid will be fixed up, only not looking so good, and some of the Cruisers will be citizens there, and the old business starts all over. Those who have and those who don't." They got news from a variety of sources. Hawkerman was by now a legend at the Lakes, and men stopped by every day to talk to him or just be seen with him. The team learned how Frumitch and the canny old historian, Nastor, had done a deal. Nastor called it a "realignment of ideologies," and what it meant was free trade between the two societies and the right for Lakesiders to enter the Pyramid to conduct business. And there would henceforward be a fairer distribution of water, albeit in a system so complicated that few could begin to make head or tail of it.

"You should have been one of the negotiators, Hawkerman!" the visitors insisted. "No one barters better."

He had the same kind of answer every time. "One on one, maybe. I stick to what I know. I spent a lifetime getting good at it. These people who want to be some kind of figure, they're putting themselves in the way of grief."

Essa's foster parents sought her out. They were escorted in by a swaggering band of Cruisers bringing gifts to Hawkerman from Frumitch, who had a well-developed eye for the politic move. Already Bonix had chosen his own future—to work for the rest of his life restoring Arcone to its former perfection. He had little to say to Essa, guilty he had not visited his adopted daughter in her time of trial. The closest he came to indicating that she still had a place in his household was when he mumbled, "If we all work together, things can be restored to how they were. We must be thankful the main cooling unit was undamaged."

It was left to Marran to say, "You must choose your own destiny, Elessa. I will support you in whatever choice you make."

Essa had been grateful and had hugged her; and had felt at the same time more apart from her than ever before. It couldn't be helped.

"I don't know what to *do*," she said to Hawkerman.

The team leader deliberated. "You're welcome to stay. For now. We'll be heading out some time, and then, well, we'd have to think again."

"Maybe I should go back to Arcone . . ."

She made it a half question. She had not yet seen the city in its semidemolished state and had no desire to, either, so she was glad when he said simply, "You can't ever go back to the Pyramid. You're known as someone who helped smash it. There's plenty would kill you for that—after they told you some fine words about justice, of course."

There was no news about Grollat. Kean and Essa had been the last people to set eyes on him, shortly after he had advised the Council that the day was lost and they should seek terms. He was almost certainly dead.

When the idea came to her, Essa acted on it. The unfathomable Commander had approved of her determination to learn about the history of Arcone, she believed. His halfway decent treatment of her was not just the product of losing a daughter, or because something in her rebellious nature had appealed to him. She made it her business to act as the clearing center for any of the records that might be found from the Archive. While the historians in Arcone gathered any found by Bleachers, Wanderers brought others to Essa, at Hawkerman's request. The piece of paper she had rescued had been totally mesmerizing—to her, anyway. So far she had showed it only to Kean, and his reaction had disappointed her.

"So?" he had said.

Only one other paper item was found and brought to her. The protective film on it had taken a beating and, torn and sodden, it revealed little to Essa. It was a picture with part of a printed caption still legible. "Mid-Season Surprise!" it read. The lettering was very regular, archaic, many centuries old. The picture seemed to be of large men wearing helmets, struggling together on a field. As far as she could see, it had nothing at all to do with the Season; it reminded her most of one of the warlike games played in the Pyramid. Keep-Ball, maybe. In a subheading on the paper, you could just make out the words "Giants Take A Tumble." Giants? The men looked big, yes, but giants? No one believed in giants. Maybe there had once been a race of bigger men and women, out beyond the valley. Strong enough to live somewhere among the gray wastes, maybe. The infuriatingly incomprehensible picture only made her more aware of her ignorance.

Driven by this frustration, she took a shortcut. She asked Hawkerman to get a message to Veramus, if he was still alive.

He was, and as anxious to keep out of trouble as usual. What he actually heard from Hawkerman was that his life was under threat if he did not cooperate with Essa, and the apprentice historian believed it, for unsolved murders were taking place daily in this time of turmoil, when men settled old scores with little fear of retribution. He diligently copied out and sent to Essa some of the information she was looking for to fill gaps in her knowledge. It wasn't much; most of the contents of the Archive were lost forever, scattered to the four corners of the valley and beyond.

When the Season calmed down, Hawkerman was off, taking only Kean and Wil with him. As far as he was concerned, it was business as usual, and he wanted to be the first to get to Skyfly's base in the Rocks. Not only had Skyfly parted him from a large quantity of valuable trading goods, but there was the rest of the flier's hoard somewhere up there. They hauled the trailer out of the Lakes in near-perfect traveling conditions, wet yet temperate, and despite being short-handed, made good time.

Without Skyfly, the balloon settlement was a hor-rifying scene. His goods were wind-scattered all over the area, and the deformed and hopeless who had been his followers were decimated by starvation and natural wastage of other kinds. Sickness and the big cats had accounted for some, and internal disputes had killed more, and there was one other, more sinister reason for the demise of several.

Spitless was still there, the only one who had made any attempt to make himself a power base, persuading two or three others to become his adherents. This group was better fed than the others.

Among the goods bartered for the balloon flight was the big ski they had found when Joe had been attacked by the Long Ones. When Spitless tried to trade with Hawkerman for this and certain other articles he especially prized, he was told, "These things were Skyfly's, and he's gone. Now they're mine again."

In the night, Hawkerman shot and killed Spitless and another man. Kean was astounded by the action until Hawkerman told him, "They had a little secret of good health. I came up on them when they were eating. It wasn't charjaw and it wasn't cats, and it once walked on two legs."

It was good to leave. Hawkerman was disappointed by the whole endeavor, and fretful. "We need to get our hands on some plastics. That's the substance that's going to be in demand."

He made them dig a cache for most of the things they had taken, some twenty miles from the Lakes. "No one's going to prospect this close to home. These items will have more value when things settle down."

And they dragged the near-empty trailer back to base. The other teams looked at them with sympathy. "Got nothing for your troubles? Isn't that the way it goes."

⁓

At last Essa had the story of Arcone's early days, and her mind was at rest. She knew something of what had happened and how the valley had come to be as it was. Wailing Joe had proved an ally and a good listener.

One calm night, two days after the team was reunited, he announced, "Elessa is going to speak."

Supper was over, and the team was together. Hawkerman, Cara, Wil, Barb, and Kean. Wailing Joe had invited
many of his acquaintances among the Wanderers to come
and learn what for hundreds of years had been Arcone's
most closely guarded secrets. On this one occasion, Hawkerman had allowed them to build a big fire, so the scene was
brightly lit.

Essa started off much too formally. "I had always wondered about the history of Arcone. About how the Pyramid
began. After all, wouldn't we all like to know how we got
here?" It did not sound at all like her, and she found herself
stammering like Veramus. "It wasn't p-permitted to know
these things, and that just made me want to know even
more."

"All you got to do is tell the story," Wailing Joe advised
with a kind of grandfatherly pride. "It's a beauty," he told
the audience. "Needs a song. I'm working on one."

So she told them what she had learned, secrets previously known only to the Bleacher aristocracy.

Many hundreds of years ago, a great civilization had
been brought to its knees by a great natural catastrophe.
This had triggered a whole series of lesser disasters, equally
mysterious, though some must have been manmade. There
was cataclysmic war, and sickness and drought ravaged the
lands. Among those who had not contracted disease, the fittest were sent to build a haven in some environment where
their infant young might be protected from ill health, secur-
ing the continuance of the society. It was hoped that genetic

experiments would produce a race better able to survive in the increasingly hard climate. After a long march and many tribulations, the valley—"The Gentle Valley"—was chosen for its water supply, and the haven was constructed, a giant pyramid they had brought with them in prefabricated sections. But the once-magnificent civilization was breaking up too fast. Marauding bands attacked the Pyramid and were beaten off, until there came an army of vandals who could not be so easily withstood. At the last, the entire adult population sealed their young children within the Pyramid and ventured out for the final battle. The defenders used chemical weapons. All perished, both the marauders and the virtuous. The last of these died within sight of the Pyramid, unwilling to venture back inside in case they spread pestilence among their children.

Over the next years in Arcone, the children grew up without tutelage. They fought among themselves as they grew to adulthood, and massive damage was done within the Pyramid. Most of the written records were destroyed. Finally there emerged a dictator among the young people, who killed those that would not follow him and drove their children out into the increasingly barren valley. This was Austan the Great. He decreed that those who remained were the Chosen Ones, whose destiny it was to preserve the Pyramid that had been bequeathed to them. Only Austan's inner circle knew that during the lawless times, the true history of their people had been all but destroyed, and in later years, only the Prime Conscience was allowed to view the few remaining fragments of the original records. It was said that none that saw them could ever again know true peace of mind.

"See—see?" Wailing Joe crowed. "I always knew it—we're just the same as they are!"

"Well, we all knew that," Hawkerman said with a small smile.

"But what we didn't know," Essa said loudly above the buzz of conversation that had started, "what we didn't know before was that the Arconians—I mean, the Bleachers—they didn't create the Pyramid. All they've done is look after it and kind of worship it. The things they can do that you can't, they learned from experimenting with what wasn't destroyed after all the elders died. No wonder they made so many disfigured people—they never really understood anything about the science of making people stronger!"

Kean had been spending much of his time scavenging for food for the team and had not heard all of the story Essa was relating. The truth was that he had feelings for her, and had neither the experience to cope with them nor any wish to express them. So he dealt with the problem by avoiding her as much as possible. He did know about something she had not yet spoken of, though.

"Tell them about the other pyramid," he said eagerly, excited by the excitement of those around him.

"Yes," Essa said. She had the priceless pieces of paper in a plastic envelope now, and carried it everywhere with her. Carefully she drew it out.

"We found this in the Archive—where they kept all the records. If you want to look at it, you'll have to come up one by one. It's very precious."

They lined up to lay eyes on the paper she held out, and many gasped when they had. Essa kept talking.

"The old civilization took its history with it. Only just like so much else, most of it was lost in the times of anarchy in the Pyramid, when no one was interested in learning. There are only a few fragments left, and this is one of them—a page from a document about our Pyramid. You'll see a picture of another pyramid on it, and it's not made of plastics. It's a place, the writing says, that was the model for our Pyramid. It's called Snefru's Bent Pyramid at Dahshur. I don't know who he was or where that is. But Arcone was originally called something else." She enunciated carefully: "Ark One."

As each Wanderer came to the front, where the firelight shone on Essa and her find, he or she saw the top page from a presentational document. It was headed with the words "The Semipermanent Ark One: Design and Build by Gonzales-Kovac Inc." Beneath that was an exploded diagram of the proposed structure, and beneath that a headline: "Fired by the Past, We Forge a Future."

And at the bottom of the page was the Bent Pyramid at Dahshur, a massive artifact emerging from a desert landscape as if it were growing from it.

Hawkerman stood up. He had not exhibited any interest in Essa's historical research until this moment. As a man of consequence, the Wanderers let him through to the front. He stared at the picture of the ancient pyramid for some time, seeing its strength and potency, and then turned and walked back to where he had been sitting.

Essa said, "Our Pyramid was just a place to live in when it was built. It wasn't a grand city. Nobody knew what Arcone meant, because it doesn't mean anything."

Hawkerman said softly to Kean, "That other place . . . that's something I would like to have seen."

Kean said, "Maybe it's still there, somewhere."

TWENTY

Essa sat hunched against the heat of the sun, her big Voyager hat low over her eyes, tending the metal cooking pot by her feet. She felt sure she was cooking faster than the greenback stew. If she looked up, what would she see after her eyes had grown used to the glare? Nothing but dusty brown everywhere; not a tree, not a shrub, not even an insect. Her mouth and lips were parched and painful as they had been for days now, and Hawkerman's orders were that she could not return inside the tent until the sun had touched the horizon. A hard taskmaster, Hawkerman. Well, if she had to, she would sit here for two days in a row, and all they would find of her would be her animal skin clothes, because the rest of her would have shriveled away.

She had been allowed to join the team. To another Arconian, it would have been plain, unremitting toil in terrible conditions, but to Essa it was deeply satisfying to have no rules to obey but those that kept you alive. She was proud to be a member of the finest team the valley had ever known . . . and she was very, very thirsty.

After the Season had finally finished in that abrupt way it had, as though it had been insulted and couldn't stay another moment, the sun had worked its usual trick of baking the muddy earth into brown concrete. It was amazing how the desert blooms had the strength to pierce it with their delicate stems. Then the topsoil had turned to dust, and the flowers had wilted, and the valley was back to normal.

Except around the Pyramid and the Lakes. Hawkerman had been right when he had said it was dangerous to be a "figure." Nastor had died in his sleep of some digestive disorder not too many weeks after the final agreement had been reached, and there were whispers of poisoning and further whispers that it was his own historians who had been responsible. About Frumitch, there were more than whispers. Both Wanderers and Cruisers spoke openly of his swollen ego and their doubt that he had struck a hard enough bargain with the defeated Bleachers. "Paid off," they said angrily. "Sold out."

The valley had lost hundreds of its population in the battle and the ensuing brutality. The eternal survivor, Wailing Joe, had words to say about that. Much against his will, he had been retired by Hawkerman to a relatively comfortable life at the Lakes. He said, "Fact is, it was needed. A general bloodletting is the kind of thing you need every hundred years or so. Cuts the number of mouths." Then he went back to composing his epic song about the valley's history. The last verse was going to be about the famous Wanderer victory at the Pyramid.

Besides Essa, Hawkerman had not yet taken on any new team members. The atmosphere in the team had changed because of the losses it had suffered. Wil, for instance. He had never been able to talk, and now he managed somehow to be quieter still. And then sometimes you would come across him making strained whispers and gurgles in his throat and smiling, and you knew he was talking to his dead sibling again. Barb took the loss of her man badly; her mouth was set hard, and you could feel the anger in her. Some nights, as they traveled, she would speak to Kean about Ax, and talk of his deeds and the ways that made him so special. Kean listened and said little, and somehow pitched his sympathy just right for her. It took Essa quite a while to realize that she was jealous of Barb. That came as a shock.

She'd tried not to think of Kean in any special way before that. He was a good companion, the friend who had come to get her out of trouble, and there was an end of it—at least, that was what she had told herself.

When the sun set, she went inside the tent and roused the team, and they brought in the food. The stew was very dry, and there was no water to drink with it. Usually Essa enjoyed the big sunset breakfast—for, as they were about to get to work, that was what it really was. There was sporadic talk, so slow and considered that you thought more deeply about even the simplest things. Tonight it was different.

Hawkerman was disturbed and angry. His plan had been to go looking for the big cache he had missed last year, in which there were plenty of plastics. It was something of an obsession with him, how he had failed before, and as before, he was in a hurry.

He said, "With a bigger team, I'd go faster."

Cara said mildly, "There would be more to feed and water."

He shot her an impatient look. "Too many women, that's what it is. Whoever heard of a team that was half women."

"You picked the team," Barb remarked. "Blame yourself."

"We'll find water," Kean said, placating Hawkerman. "We always do."

"Sure. We always do," he retorted sardonically. "Until the day we don't."

As they traveled that night, they found no waterholes and no desert wardens.

At dawn, Hawkerman called Kean to the front of the trailer and walked with him a little way. Their throats were being sandpapered raw by lack of water, and it was hard to talk.

"See out there?" Hawkerman croaked. "Sand. I steered us wrong."

"Yeah. Do we rest up? There's no strength left in the team."

"One hot day lying around and maybe we'd find it hard to move again. That's what happens. You try to rouse yourself, and you don't quite make it. So you lie there. You're still lying there same time next year."

"Where do we go? We can't go into the sand, and we know what's behind us. Nothing."

"Maybe. Think this way: in one direction, there will be water. We'll take a couple of hours here. I need to think."

For some reason, Essa was cheerful. Kean put it down to dehydration: temporary madness, like in a greenback. "Why are we stopping?" she asked with a kind of gaiety.

"It's not for long."

"What about getting water?"

"We have to rest up and get what strength we can. We might have one more day in us. We better had."

"I thought we were going on to get water. I was looking forward to it."

"You calm down. I'll do your jobs for you, if you want. You're burning up, and it isn't even light yet."

"But we have to keep going! There's water!"

"Where is there water?" he asked patiently.

"Out there. I was looking forward to it. I'm so thirsty."

She was pointing dead ahead, to where the color of the ground faded to yellow.

Kean shook his head. "That's sand. You're still new to this." Then he added, because he liked her so much, "I'm sorry we didn't do better by you."

"There's water out there." She stated it as plain fact. Kean made his way back to Hawkerman.

"Essa says there's water. Out in the sands."

"What would she know about it."

"I think she might know something. She has this feeling."

"She's ignorant about being a Wanderer. You like her, so you let yourself be persuaded."

"I heard it in her voice," Kean persisted. "Look—it depends how bad you think our circumstances are."

Hawkerman gave him a long stare. "They're bad."

Kean said, "Bad enough to look for water in the sand?"

They stood there together, silent, in the Wanderer way.

Hawkerman turned to the rest of the team. He called, "Pick up the trailer. We're moving on."

Three hours later, well into the morning, well into the sand, they were near collapse. Essa staggered along at the front of the trailer, leading them. Optimism had died long ago. There was nothing to do but move on till they fell and could move no more.

Then there was something different on the blank horizon. Kean saw it first, with that famed eyesight of his.

A little later he said, "Desert wardens."

It was. A low-lying stand of the cacti growing in the barren landscape where they shouldn't be, young and tender. The team gathered the last reserves of their strength and hauled the trailer all the long way to the carriers of life.

When the first water had been extracted and drunk in careful quantity, Hawkerman went to Essa. He cautioned her gently, "Not too much. Not too fast."

She felt his hand on her shoulder.

He said, "I do believe we have ourselves a Waterboy."

$\backsim$

It confused Kean. He had felt protective about Essa, and now she had respect of a kind he had always wished for himself. For there was no doubt she was a Waterboy. She had the gift. Hawkerman had set her a series of tests, letting her guide the team when water began to run short, and she led them to it every time, often across great distances. They were all empowered by the talent she had; with water no longer a problem, they were a truly great team, invulnerable.

She asked herself *why* and *how*, and found no answers. It was an affinity she had with the essential element, and that was all you could say about it.

Not only did they find the cache, but ten days before that, they came to the place where Wailing Joe had had his narrow escape from the Long Ones. Smoke was used to drive out more of the snakes who had gathered and some serious excavations were made. There was another of those peculiar long skis down there, and some coiled steel springs, as well as more common bits and pieces.

The famous cache itself was a work of many days and nights. As they dug deeper, it became plain that the encampment that had stood there when the climate had been more temperate had been a fairly sizeable one. The yearly Seasons had buried it so deep there was no calculating how many years it could be mined profitably. On this visit, plastic panels were the articles Hawkerman most desired, the larger the better. Packing the trailer became a finely judged exercise, and he resolved to rebury the single awkwardly shaped ski and unearth it again on another visit.

Kean said, "I want that." He hardly knew it till he said it.

Hawkerman grunted, "You've earned it, Kean," and repacked the trailer again without further questions.

That night was a rest night. Kean and Hawkerman stayed awake, and Hawkerman nodded for Kean to follow him out of the tent.

It was a still, warm night, one of the few that occurred after the Season had departed.

"What's with you, Kean?" Hawkerman inquired.

For many hours, Kean had asked himself the same question. "I've been thinking about transport," he said at last.

"Yes?"

"The wind."

"Don't get much wind except during the Season. And that ski thing, that wouldn't travel well out here."

"If we had the other one . . . there's the Big White."

"What's the matter? Tired of being a Wanderer? Or tired of life?"

"You said yourself, nothing's going to change here."

"It might." Hawkerman allowed himself a smile. "You could do something yourself to change things. Ever think about that?"

"I used to think it might be good to live in the Pyramid. Two seconds inside it and I knew I was wrong. I don't have any interest in it at all now, or what happens at the Lakes, either. But the idea of getting across the Big White, that does interest me, from the top of my head right down to my feet."

"That's youth for you. Greedy, never satisfied." But Hawkerman did not seem at all irritated when he said it. He looked out into the night. "You want to tackle the Big White, you need a Waterboy. No way without one."

"That's it," Kean said awkwardly. "That's the thing. But . . . I couldn't take her—it wouldn't be right. Wouldn't be fair to the team."

"Have you asked her?"

"I thought you and me should talk first. I don't want to hurt the team."

"The team needs rebuilding," Hawkerman said slowly. "I knew that, and I just didn't want to do it until I plain had to. See, Kean, that girl, she belongs to you as much as she does to the team—more, probably. You have a kind of history together."

"Yes," said Kean, encouraged. "That's true, isn't it."

Hawkerman remarked dryly, "Only thing is, she belongs most to herself. You'll have to ask her, not me."

"Yes. I thought I should ask you first, that's all."

"No, you didn't. You're scared to ask her, 'case she says no. It's natural."

Kean protested that he had no such worry. Hawkerman smiled disbelievingly and started back toward the tent. He said over his shoulder, so quietly that Kean could hardly hear him, "She'll go with you. All you got to do is ask."

∽

They were on their way back to the Lakes, and only half the year was gone. This year there was to be no second expedition.

One evening Hawkerman gave the team his reasons. "I got to train new men into the team. And besides, there's something near the Lakes that Kean wants to get his hands on—isn't that right, Kean?"

He meant the other long ski, which they had buried; he was teasing after his fashion, and Kean felt himself growing hot. He still hadn't asked Essa if she would go with him on the attempt to cross the Big White. Every day he was going to speak to her about it, and every day he hadn't. Why not? He couldn't understand it, when they got on so well. Each morning when he woke, it seemed ridiculous that he still hadn't broached the subject, and as the minutes passed, an invisible impediment presented itself, a barrier so strong that no amount of willpower could breach it.

That night there was one of those rare thick frosts on the ground, and the team took time out from traveling to scrape up the ice for drinking water. Essa took the initiative and attached herself to Kean, making sure they drifted out of earshot of the others. As they scraped away and filled a plastic box with dirty frost, she asked with humorous curiosity, "What's the big secret? What's this thing you want that Hawkerman isn't telling us about?"

That was all it took—someone else to make the first move. He began telling her about the skis, and how after his headlong dash in the attack wagon, he had seen a way of making a fast start on a trek over the Big White. Then of course he had to tell her of the others who had tried to get out of the valley over the many years, and how no one knew for sure if anyone had been successful—except maybe that man who'd ridden the bizarre animal . . . and . . . and there was no way he could avoid speaking of the essential condition for attempting such a journey: you had to have a Waterboy.

The rest of the team had gone back to the trailer. They were alone out here.

"You thought—what? I'd come with you?"

"I thought . . . I thought I could ask you."

"And are you asking me?"

"Yes. I am."

"But you haven't."

"I did—just now."

"I could die, most like, if I do what you want me to—and you can't even say, 'Will you please come with me across the Big White?'"

"'Please'?"

"Certainly 'please.' You'd have to say please."

It was absurd. He couldn't do it.

She said, "I'm cold out here. Just say it."

Well, put that way . . . They couldn't stay out here for-ever, and she *did* look like she was getting very cold.

"Yes . . . um . . . Essa. Would you—please—come with me and go across the Big White? If we can, that is."

"Yes," she said.

TWENTY-ONE

They told Hawkerman. He said, "You talk about it some more, between yourselves. I won't tell the others just yet. You could change your mind. That's the point of having a mind—to make rational choices."

"But do you think we could make it?" Essa asked, subdued by his downbeat response.

"I don't have any information on the subject—how can I tell? One thing you should consider: you'll need someone else along with you. Otherwise you might as well lie down and die right here."

He smiled at their disquiet, and Kean misinterpreted it. "You might come with us yourself?"

Hawkerman shook his head. "It's not the kind of odds I play."

"You were the one who made the attack on the Pyramid work. That was against all the odds."

"It was necessary."

"No," Kean said positively. "You did it because it was the right thing to do. Because your brother would have died for nothing if you hadn't."

"That's a very fine way of looking at killing people. A lot of them innocent of bad intent."

"Well, it had to be done."

"Well, maybe it did, at that. Did you ever consider that if the Bleachers had destroyed the Lakes instead of the other way around, I'd have no one left to trade with?"

"That wasn't the reason."

"Well, it's the only good reason *I* can think of. We're getting off the point here."

You didn't get anywhere when you tried to unearth good intentions in Hawkerman.

The following weeks were difficult for Kean and Essa. They wanted to be together, and they wanted to avoid talk about it. Cara sensed the new feeling between them and put it down to, well, just what they did not want it to be put down to. It was difficult for them, and all the time they had this new inner nervousness, because they were going to risk their lives.

The return trip to the Lakes was uneventful by Wanderer standards. Back in the settlement, they discovered the Bleachers had set up several trading posts, and Hawkerman reveled in haggling with such inexperienced dealers. With no time to manufacture them, plastics were in high demand, as he had suspected, and he did well, bartering goods mostly for food notes, which the

Bleachers guaranteed to exchange for victuals at specified periods of time.

There was a new order forming. Plenty of Lakesiders were employed helping with the Pyramid's reconstruction, and the line between the two societies was blurring. Wailing Joe had been keeping an eye on things. "It mostly goes one way—as in, the Lakesiders working for the Bleachers. That's where it's all going to go wrong."

"They have a sense of purpose in the Pyramid, that's the difference," Hawkerman observed.

On the plains a few nights later, they dug up the second big ski. On the way there, Hawkerman asked Kean and Essa if they had changed their minds. They had not. As the team settled down in the tent to sleep out the day, Hawkerman asked for their attention.

"Kean and Essa are going to try to cross the Big White," he said matter-of-factly. "And I am going to help them all I can."

It was the first time he had said that. Kean was pleased right through. It made the perilous undertaking seem possible.

Hawkerman went on, "They will need another team member. Out of us, or from another source. Cara won't go, so of the people here, that leaves Wil or Barb. Think about it."

Cara said, "How do you know I wouldn't go?"

Hawkerman answered, "Because I couldn't let you."

She smiled one of her rare smiles. "That's the nicest thing you've said in years."

He was embarrassed, though not displeased.

"Anyway. Have yourselves a think."

That seemed to be that for now, until Barb declared suddenly, "I'll go. Happy to."

Essa went red and felt furious. Said nothing. It was Cara who put the question. "Why would you want to, Barb?"

"Because Ax died."

It seemed reason enough. Kean knew the etiquette of the situation. "We'd be glad of your company, Barb. You'd make a difference."

Barb thought aloud, "There wouldn't be a team leader. Too few of us. We'd take decisions jointly."

"I wouldn't want it any other way," Kean answered. "Essa?"

"Yes . . ." And all at once, she was comfortable with the idea. In some ways, better a woman than another man. Barb was no threat. She was remote and suffering and needed to make the journey for her own reasons—it was nothing to do with Kean. Essa got up and went to Barb and touched her shoulder. "There's no one I'd be more pleased to have along."

It was the right thing to say and do. Barb smiled and it was done.

Hawkerman pondered. "Shame Cancher's dead. We need some skills to make a wagon. Old Joe's past it."

Everyone sat up and began to talk, oblivious to the growing heat in the tent. Unable to speak, Wil listened enthusiastically, and smiled and nodded vehemently to make his own contributions.

Hawkerman thought they had better keep the venture to themselves. "The ideal is, no one even notices. We 'specially don't let anyone know there's a Waterboy in the valley. People would tell us Essa has to stay for the good of everyone else."

"Secret is best," Barb agreed.

Hawkerman went on, "If you're using the winds to get you going, we got about three months to prepare. I think for the Season we better find ourselves a base away from the Lakes."

Cara came in with, "No one knows how big the Big White is. It's not a wagon you want, it's a trailer—only purpose-built."

They talked for some minutes more, building a picture of this wonder vehicle on long skis, with optional wheels. They were a team, pulling together to achieve something. It was a good feeling, and for that time in the stifling tent, the nervousness left Kean and Essa.

It came back, however: a haunting fear that you could easily confuse with a premonition of failure.

There were plenty of men to choose from when it came to picking new recruits for the team. In the battle at the Pyramid, many crews had lost members. Whole new teams had formed and gone out, raw and argumentative. Other Wanderers were more cautious about their futures, and Hawkerman could have seen fifty more men than he did, if he had not made it a rule that he would consider no one who was defecting from a still-functioning team. He was looking for three to join, and the first two were easy enough to decide on: Creaser and Wideboy.

Creaser was from one of the disbanded teams, a tall, lugubrious man of thirty-odd, known for his amazing stamina. Wideboy was a novice not yet twenty years of age, and he was just what his name said, *wide*, and the widest thing of all was his grin. Hawkerman liked to have one big man on the team, and this good-natured hulk fit the bill and then some. Kean took to him at once.

After that, candidates were much of a muchness. Hawkerman was offered bribes, and he had to fight and beat one man who took offense at being thought unworthy of the team.

"I've had enough of this," Hawkerman sighed as Cara dabbed away at a cut above his eyebrow. "I'm not big enough or young enough anymore to go scuffling with every poor fool who has a grievance."

So temporarily he gave up looking for team members, and instead began looking for someone who could help with designing and building Kean's trailer.

He wanted the very best man, and that turned out to be one of the least popular traders in the whole of the Lakes.

For some reason, Hardly-There had escaped renaming since being born tiny, two months premature. Possibly no one could be bothered, including Hardly-There himself. That he had survived his early entry into the world was no surprise when you knew him; his name could have been abbreviated very simply to "Hard." A chunky nugget of a man, he had a crabby, unbending nature, and even Hawkerman could not best him in a deal. Since the death of his notoriously ferocious woman in the fighting at the Pyramid, he was worse-natured than ever, although the private joke among his neighbors was that it should have made him cheerier.

Hardly-There was as much an engineer as a trader, buying and refashioning items made from any material you could find in the valley. For a high price, he had secretly advised Fireface on the making of his attack wagons, as Hawkerman learned.

Kean was present at the interview with him. It took an unexpected turn.

"Why do you want this kind of trailer, anyway?" Hardly-There asked sullenly, outside the well-appointed shed where he slept with his goods. It was a dull red evening, and there was a hum of activity all over the Lakes.

"My business."

"Silence costs extra."

"We'll bear that in mind as we deal."

Hardly-There tried to put that moment off. "Got your team yet?" He added caustically, "The best in the valley?"

"One short. Going to leave it at that."

Changing the topic of conversation, Hardly-There said, "You've got these skis, you say. Constructed solid? Not welded from two pieces?"

"Solid. Kean said they'd need to be, for strength."

"That's the pale-skinned boy of yours."

"Yes."

"Another hero," Hardly-There sneered.

"Good man to have on a team," was Hawkerman's neutral reply.

It appeared that Hardly-There had run out of words for a second or two. Until he said in an uncomfortable whisper, "Take me into your team, and you get the work for nothing." He waited. "Think about it."

Hawkerman thought about it, thought about what he knew of Hardly-There.

Hardly-There said, "I need something new. I do, too. I'd try real hard to fit in."

Hawkerman thought about the composition of his team, tried to visualize Hardly-There working alongside the others. Thought of his skills.

He nodded. "You're in."

The team was complete.

⌇

A search lasting several weeks turned up a hidden campsite near the Big White where they could build the craft and launch it on the winds when they came. Around five hundred yards from the start of the bleached desert, the Rocks tumbled down in a welter of gargantuan rubble, honeycombed with caves. In the biggest of these was a natural chimney, so they could feed and heat themselves with some comfort.

There was a reason no one had ever set up home here; it was the habitation of several families of the big cats. Driving them out took another two weeks and was about the most dangerous exercise you could undertake. It had the consequence of knitting the new team together. At first Essa felt sorry for the cats, but when you saw them close up, long and scarred and liquid-muscled, and staring at you with cold golden anger, you quickly accepted them as a life force who saw you only as moving food.

Where there was such a large concentration of animals there must be water, too, and Essa found it only half a day's march away, well-nigh hidden in another tumbledown confluence of rocks.

Eaten for food themselves, the big cats did not taste good, as the new Wanderer, Hardly-There, discovered after they had killed a few.

Hawkerman said, "They got things to do, we got things to do. Only kill if you have to. That's their way, and it should be ours, too."

Hardly-There thought that was a puny, soft-hearted approach and advocated that they slaughter each and every one of the beasts and let them rot. Hawkerman told him, "If a creature can find a way to live out here, it deserves to go on living," and then got Kean to talk to Hardly-There. "See if you can get through to him. If you can't, he's out. Well—soon as the trailer's built."

They went everywhere in twos because of the threat of the cats, which might at any moment launch themselves from behind a boulder. Kean and Hardly-There were at work shifting smaller rocks in order to clear a flat area with a natural windbreak, where the trailer could be assembled. Hardly-There labored with a will until Kean told him to stop.

"Why? We could finish this today."

"You don't use all your strength. Keep some back so you stay sharp. Use too much and you sleep too heavy and drink too much water. We've got time enough."

Hardly-There did not like taking orders from Kean, but they sat awhile. Kean told him a few tales about Hawkerman and his methods, and then he said, "Hawkerman never wastes energy. So he's not going to tell you when you overstep the mark. The way you'll find out is when he asks you to leave. Every waking minute you've got to show him you fit in with us."

"Well," Hardly-There grunted unwillingly, "if I was in his place, I suppose that's the way I'd handle it, too." It came hard, but he said it. "Thanks, Kean."

They talked a little more, about Kean's exploits in the Pyramid. Hardly-There was impressed even if he tried not to show it. He asked, "Why is Hawkerman helping you like this? It costs plenty, and it takes all this time—why would he do it?"

Kean had been over that in his mind. "I'm a team member. We've spent a lot of time together . . . Hardly-There, I'll tell you. I don't know."

Hardly-There reverted to type. "Maybe you done something, and he wants you eaten by vultures. If they fly over the Big White, that is. If I was a vulture, I wouldn't."

Essa herself still had to concentrate on fitting in and doing the right thing. She was not yet as physically tough as the others, and she hoped her powers of endurance would not let them down when they crossed the Big White. Or tried to . . .

Secret trips were made to the Lakes for materials, and they accumulated in the cave under Hardly-There's supervision. "Dimensions, strength, weight . . ." He would mutter these or other such keywords to himself as he designed the craft in his head. One night he required the three voyagers to line up so he could lift them, one by one, to gauge their weight. He was pleased with *that*. "No bodyweight at all—when you think there's three of them."

Aluminum did not come cheap. Hawkerman remarked, "This is going to be the most expensive trailer ever built."

Hardly-There joked, "Let's hope it gets years of use, then."

When construction started, Hawkerman sent Essa to the Pyramid.

∽

Wideboy went with her as bodyguard. She would rather it was Kean. Hawkerman said, "The two of you together? It would get some Bleacher folk worked up till they could murder." So Wideboy it was: his first time inside the city. Essa felt bad, because it had been Cara, not she, who had suggested she see her foster parents. It would be for the last time; Essa couldn't refuse.

They stopped off at the Lakes, where you got tokens that were like permits to enter the city. As yet, there was no charge for the privilege. They timed the journey to arrive at dawn. Essa gasped as Arcone materialized through the night sky. Half of it was missing.

Not half. A third, maybe. In order to withstand the approaching Season, the sections that were hopelessly wrecked had been removed in their entirety, and the inner walls in these areas had been shored up tight. No longer was Semipermanent Ark One a beautiful structure. The hope was that next year, the original shape would be restored, no matter how clumsily, so long as it was strong.

A young Pacifier, surely underage for the job, led them up to the new apartment occupied by Bonix and Marran.

It was a dingy one-room affair. Marran looked tired. She said, "You didn't have to come."

So she understood how things had changed between them. What she did not know was that in all probability, this was the last time she would ever lay eyes on the girl she had brought up as her daughter. Her main worry today was that she had no food to offer them.

Essa said, "Don't worry about food. Wideboy eats too much, anyway!"

Wideboy grinned.

Marran took them on a tour of the Pyramid as they looked for Bonix. Everywhere they went, Wideboy was awed and amazed by the splendor of the place.

"It looked better before," Essa said dryly.

Bonix was working in the Middle Chamber, a small figure in its great space, and his face lit up when he saw Essa. That was unexpected, and moving.

He was fervent in his satisfaction with the work he was doing. Wideboy quickly tired of the conversation as Bonix got Essa to admire—as an expert in her own right—the quality of the repairs he was engaged in.

"Of course, it can't look the same, using temporary measures as we have to, but—believe it or not—the acoustics are even better than they used to be!"

He took Wideboy to be more than just a companion and told him, "Essa must bring you to an Evening of Beauty here—next year, perhaps. You will see the sweetness of our life in Arcone!"

All in all, her farewell turned out to be more *hello* than *goodbye*. There was nothing she could do about it.

Marran asked her, "Are you happy?"

"I think so. I feel very alive. Maybe that's the same thing. Are you still painting?"

"No. Not yet. One day, maybe."

"I wanted to ask you—has there been any word of the Commander?"

"Grollat? No. Now he is being blamed for our reversal. It's always the way, isn't it. Blame the absent. If he is alive, he is wise to keep out of sight."

"I don't think he cared whether Arcone triumphed or not."

Marran said sharply, "He was a fearsome man. I hope he's dead."

Essa could not picture him dead. He was the kind of person who went on forever, somewhere.

She and Wideboy left the Pyramid shortly afterward. It was hot; looking back, Arcone shimmered in the heat haze, dreamlike.

TWENTY-TWO

The Season was due, and the trailer was finished.

It was low to the ground, a sliver of aluminum with a single broad cockpit at the back. Cara and Wil had made new tie-down Voyager hats for them, and leather gauntlets. While the winds blew, they would be traveling in the heat of the day. There were storage bays in the belly of the craft to hold water sacks and food, and when asleep on the ground on their leather pallets, the little team would be insulated by Arconian technology, boxed in by a buckle-on skirt for the trailer that consisted of heatproof panels from the black market at the Lakes.

The sail was made of five skins from the big cats. Metal eyelets had been stitched into it, so it could be raised on the mast on leather lines. The mast itself was a short steel cross. Four wheels were lashed to the back of the trailer, and they spoiled its natural elegance, as did the two sharp steering poles.

Hardly-There said gloomily, "Why steer at all, if you don't even know where you're going?"

The skis were much longer than the vehicle itself and cushioned by a primitive suspension system suggested by the steel springs that had been found with them. "Theory," Hardly-There said. "The length of the skis reduces the bumps. Never use wheels when you're going at speed. They'll strike and flip you over."

Barb did not say much. But they could tell she was still glad to be going on the venture, when they saw her satisfaction as she ran her hands along the smooth aluminum of the trailer.

Kean and Essa worked hard, and thought about the voyage every waking moment, and grew more and more anxious. He said to her once, "You can still change your mind," just as Hawkerman had said it to him.

"Oh, now, that's not fair," Essa retorted angrily. "If you're going, I'm going. But if you don't want to, just say so—don't leave it all up to me."

"No. I mean, I do want to go. It's the same with me—if you're going, I'm going."

They talked to Hawkerman. He took them away from the cave, and they sat by the trailer itself. In the rocks up above them, one of the long gray cats was noisily eating a medium-size lizard, the staple diet of the felines. The cat choked momentarily and gave out one of those deep echoing coughs. Hawkerman had got it right, and the team's presence was now accommodated by the big predators. You still watched your back, though.

Kean and Essa told him how they were feeling.

"You've got doubts," he said quietly. "That's natural. Just remember, there's no shame if you don't go."

"We've got to go now," Kean agonized. "We'd have wasted all this effort otherwise. It's cost you so much, too."

"That doesn't matter. The point is, you can't take this thing on unless your hearts are right in it."

"We'd look like such fools," Essa said.

"Ah, get that one out of your heads—*that* doesn't help you. What you do, now the danger is near and you're fearful, is remember why you wanted to do this thing in the first place. Then you balance one thing against the other and see what comes out on top."

In the state they were in, they could not remember why the idea had ever attracted them at all. So he told them. "There's something out there. No knowing what it is. It might be a race of men who run as fast as greenbacks . . . You're young and curious, and you have this feeling that you need to know, and you sense that together you could make it through. Men have tried before you, and my belief is that some of them made it. And there's this for you to consider: between you, you're the perfect Wanderer. Kean—you don't burn, and you can go all day, and you see better than any mortal man ever did before. Ask me, you're the result they wanted when they did those experiments in the Pyramid, all those years back. As for Essa, well, you've got the greatest talent of all. You're a Waterboy."

He had rarely said so much all in one go before, and he wasn't finished.

"I don't know what we're here for." He sighed. "Except maybe to look after each other now and then. But every one of us, sometime in our lives, says, 'There's got to be more than *this*—what I can see here around me,' and it nags at us. If you've got that disease on you now, then you'll go. And you might just see something new."

Kean felt Essa's hand gripping into his arm, and it felt good, if a little painful. There would be three of them, in it together, and there was more to the world than this one enormous valley. Had to be.

"We're going," he announced. "Isn't that right, Essa?"

"No doubt about it," she said.

Hawkerman nodded slowly. "All right, then. If you see wonders and prosper—don't thank me. And if you should find yourselves lying out there dying, and you've seen nothing but sand . . . same thing applies." He got up and added laconically, "Be a hell of a waste of a Waterboy, though."

∽

The Season was late. It sent some clouds along, and the moment they appeared, the team loaded up the speed trailer and rolled it out onto the flatlands. Kean, Barb, and Essa stood by to jump in. The light wind dropped, and there was a short shower, and that was all. Over the next days, the sky darkened, and still the winds did not come. They moved

Hawkerman's trailer to stand next to Kean's, and set up camp on the edge of the Big White. They would head out as soon as it became possible, to make full use of the Season's wind power. The gales should not blow at full strength immediately.

It was a period of waiting. Kean came back to the camp one evening with sad-eyed Creaser. They'd been replenishing stocks from the waterhole. Creaser went on to find Wil; they were having a stone-throwing competition, like kids. It had gone on for days. Kean went into the tent. Cara was alone in there, mending a leather waistcoat. Kean wondered about the weather conditions and went outside to take a look, for the hundredth time. Was it optimism, or were the clouds beginning move about up there?

He ducked back into the tent and threw himself down on his back. The action was so abrupt that Cara missed a stitch.

"Be careful!" she snapped.

"Sorry."

"No—I'm sorry," she said quickly. "I know it's hard for you."

"Well. Not much longer now. I hope."

"They'd better get back soon," she worried.

"Yes."

"It'll be all right when you're on your way."

"I know."

Now she had started to talk, she wanted to go on. "Sometimes I wish we were going with you. All this change around here. It's disturbing."

"Yes."

"I think you should know—and I'm sure it hasn't been said—we're going to miss you, Hawkerman and me."

Kean sat up. "Cara . . ."

"Yes?"

"I've had such a fine life with you. It was good of you to take me in when I was small. You didn't have to."

"Well, that's Hawkerman for you."

"What?"

"Just when you think you know him through and through, he does the unexpected."

"But . . . it was your idea, wasn't it?"

"My idea?" She was patently amazed.

"Hawkerman told me you were the one who said I should be looked after by the team. He told me."

She looked at Kean with a quiet smile in her eyes. "Oh. Did he."

There was a noise like a shot going off, and one side of the tent began to vibrate strongly.

"It's started," Kean realized.

He stood up. "So it was Hawkerman."

Cara dropped her pieces of leather and got up, too. "Yes."

Outside the winds settled into a steady pushing; nothing too dramatic. And here was the team, gathering.

"It's now!" Hawkerman shouted. "You get in now!"

And suddenly, there was so much Kean wanted to say, and he no longer had the time. Everything was urgent movement. The water sacks in his trailer were topped up to the brim; the craft was realigned to face the center of the white horizon, the folds of the sail were rearranged so that it came up without snagging. Barb got into the cockpit and stowed her bow. She was still getting comfortable when Essa landed beside her and squirmed over to make room for Kean.

"Line her up!" Hardly-There called, and the rest of the team grabbed onto the trailer so that it kept pointing straight.

Kean was scrambling into the cockpit, inadvertently kicking both Essa and Barb. They did not notice in their excitement. Of all people, it was Hardly-There who had tears in his eyes at the moment of departure. Sad to lose the trailer he'd designed? Where was Hawkerman? It was all happening so fast . . .

The team leader made his way to the side of the cockpit. He reached over Barb and Kean to ruffle Essa's hair. On the other side of the trailer, Cara was passing their hats to them.

Hawkerman squeezed Barb's shoulder. Then he held out his hand to Kean, who took it and gripped it hard. It was their last communication, and he used the grip to say what words could not. Their hands held onto each other for a long moment.

Hawkerman let go.

Kean jammed his hat onto his head and tightened the strap.

"You all hold on," Hawkerman cried to the team, and he and Wil hauled up the sail double-quick and clipped the lines to the holding rings behind the cockpit.

The wind was easy. It was all easy.

"Let her free!" Hawkerman called. *"Now!"*

They were off, slowly enough for Wil to run beside them for a few yards. He smiled and grimaced his good wishes, clenching his fists in encouragement.

The sail became round with air, and they picked up speed. Wil fell behind.

It had all been so quick. Kean had not said goodbye as he wanted to, and now they were so tightly packed in the cockpit that he could not even turn his head to look behind him. Could not get a last look at the team as the trailer slid away. Could not see Hawkerman and Cara standing side-by-side, waving anyway.

∽

The craft was well-balanced and traveled smoothly. The white sands around them shone iridescently, glowing under the thunderous evening skies. Already that was all there was: dark sky and white sand.

The rain tore in from behind them; they could hear it well before it hit. Then it was like being bashed in the back by a giant wet hand, and the trailer really took off, accelerating with astounding swiftness. The gales pushed it hard into the ground, and the skis skidded over the soaking sand with a hungry licking sound.

Hardly-There's theory about the length of the skis proved correct. The trailer shot over bumps and kept a steady course. The ground grew wetter. Kean and his crew grew wetter. It was impossible to see through the wild cascade of rain, impossible even to know whether night had set in yet. It was good to have another human body tight beside you in the soaking black maelstrom on the Big White.

∽

Twenty-four hours later, time and motion and the roaring elements were still all mixed up, and still they charged along. In the cockpit, their heads nodded low, lolled with tiredness, and banged against one another.

Eventually they were so numb they were not conscious of movement at all, just bitterly cold and wet and aching to the bone. The trailer sped on, an aluminum arrow speeding through a second night on the desert.

Before dawn, the rain stopped, and the wind dropped below gale force. They could shout to one another. There was nothing to say, though.

"Are you all right?"

"Yes—are you?"

A second day on the Big White. The wind craft powered on. Nothing to see but flat white sand. They ate little and drank sparingly. Barb managed to get some sleep; Kean and Essa faced front and traveled on dully with eyes slitted or closed, neither awake nor asleep.

Near dusk they had one of those strange lulls in the prevailing weather and could get out of the trailer. The sand was like fire underfoot.

Within an hour the winds got up again and drove them steadily across the level ground. The accompanying rain did not return, however, until the middle of the night. There came a time when competing gales battered the trailer from all sides, sending it zigzagging—almost turning over—until it was blasted to a swaying stop, its sail flapping uncontrollably. When they were moving forward again, Kean had to wait for a glimpse of the moon and stars before he knew the wind had resumed its regular direction, or something close to it. It was not as strong as it had been: the trailer was moving much less quickly.

By morning they had finally outrun the rain.

By midafternoon, it seemed that they had outrun the wind itself. The sail sagged. The trailer slowed down further over the course of an hour, until it was only inching along.

They came to a stop under a burnished sky.

All around, the Big White. Flat and featureless, and glaring so hard that even Kean's eyes hurt.

"Out," he gasped hoarsely. "Rest up."

It had become hard to move. They were stuck fast together by habit and exhaustion. He urged them on. "Come on. Something to eat. And drink."

One of the storage compartments had taken a knock and spilled its load of water. There was no telling how much this might cost them. All three of them had headaches. They arranged the thermal skirt on the trailer and crawled underneath it with their thick leather pallets.

"Tell me we've only got a couple more days of this," Essa whispered.

"No one knows. We know it ends somewhere, but we don't know its shape." Kean breathed slowly so he didn't scorch his lungs. "A different route might be quicker—who knows? We're going straight, anyway."

Essa couldn't help doubting his skills, and hid from her more experienced companions the fear she had. That dread that, if viewed in the moonlight from a long way above, their tracks might be seen to veer consistently to one side or the other. The fear that they were describing a circle in the endless sand.

After a bit of food, they sank into the familiar sleep that was like a sickness.

When they awoke at nightfall, they became aware of the utter silence, something greater and emptier than you encountered in even the most desolate places in the valley. It made conversation hard; you felt you had to have something really important to say if you were going to break this stillness.

So it was without much talk that they stowed the sail and tied on the lines to haul the trailer by hand.

The ensuing days followed the pattern Barb and Kean had known all their lives; that familiar routine of daytime rest and night travel. Through the day, the sun seemed hotter and bigger with every passing hour. When the sand became less hard-packed, they changed the skis for the wheels. An argument: keep the skis or leave them?

Barb said harshly, "Leave them. The wind blows one way, and we won't be going back."

Kean said there could still be high winds coming along to help them sometime. They took the time to strap the skis onto the side of the vehicle.

Attaching the wheels did not make the going much easier.

It slowed you down, the Big White. It wanted you to stay forever.

TWENTY-THREE

It slowed you down, the Big White. The sand grew finer and softer, and the trailer more unwieldy as a consequence. There was no sign of water, or plant or animal life. No albatross sailed the wide sky; they had not even seen an insect. Essa abandoned her fantasy that one morning they would see the ancient Bent Pyramid silhouetted on the horizon. There was all-too-plainly nothing here.

They were on the last two water bags. It was hard to ration them when you knew their contents were evaporating in the heat minute by minute.

Barb said, "Waterboy, you're going to have to do your thing."

Essa said, "I can't. I don't create it—I only sense when it's there. And . . ."

"And it isn't," Kean finished for her.

Essa was suffering worse than the other two, and he was concerned for her. Already she had almost no pulling power when it came to shifting the trailer along. He wouldn't let her ride it yet, though.

⌒

When they first saw the line of dunes rising out of the sand, all across the horizon, blocking their progress, they were stimulated out of their torpor. It was impossible to tell how big they were, and in any case, it took two days to reach them, and one water bag. The sandy hills rose up for six hundred feet, sculpted in graceful curves with razor-sharp ridges curling this way and that. The trailer bogged down immediately when they began the climb. Day had gone, and the moon was brilliant in the sky.

Essa said faintly, "Do we need the trailer?"

Kean asked, "Why do you say that?"

"It could be the end of the Big White on the other side—don't you think?"

It was worth a look, anyway. Kean left the others and struggled up the sandy cliff, sinking ankle-deep into it. Streams and rivulets of the fine sand ran down behind him.

At the sharp line of the summit, where small winds argued about which should prevail, he looked back at the women. They heard him shout, and hope flared for just a second.

"It's incredible!"

"What?" Barb called back.

"It gets lower. There's a massive drop down to get on ground level again."

He picked out a route to make the descent to a lower level of the Big White. They used the skis to get the trailer up the dunes. It took a day. Going down the other side took half a night. The skis had a tendency to bury themselves, and the wheels went back on. They staggered down the steep inclines, slewing sideways, almost overturning the trailer. It was lucky the vehicle was so light. Even so, there were long minutes when they were digging it out from where it had driven itself too deep. At the bottom, they were so tired they got under the trailer without even fixing the heat paneling.

When they surfaced from sleep in the late afternoon, the scale of what they'd come down from hit them. On this side, the dunes were mountainous.

"You know why?" Kean said. They didn't. "There's some reason that the wind changes round about here. To build these hills, it mostly has to go the other way."

To him it seemed they had achieved something in reaching this demarcation point. Before nightfall, he felt differently. They'd traveled two hours. Behind them, the sand mountains towered into the sky, and ahead of them, the Big White went on and on. Lower, maybe, but just the same.

Unending.

༄

Essa rode in the trailer now. She was very light in spite of her leather clothes, as Kean discovered when he lifted her into the cockpit.

Barb let her have the last of the water, the sip she herself was due. They hauled onward across the sand. Halfway through the night, Kean heard Essa whimpering or maybe calling in the cockpit. He was pushing, Barb was pulling, so he was the closest to Essa. He called to make a halt and went to her.

She said in a painful whisper, "Water."

"We don't have any," he told her, sick to his heart. He had killed her. He had killed them all.

"Go left. Water," she whispered.

⁓

The miniature cacti were nearly spherical and a pale yellow in color, with lime stripes on them. They did not stand out much from their surroundings, and without Essa's directions, the little team would certainly have passed them by in the day, let alone when it was dark. They were not desert wardens, yet they shared the vital characteristic: they stored water. The taproots were like wire and must have gone down way below those of a warden. Cut open, the cacti tasted bitter. Had they been poisonous, the crew of the trailer would not have minded. Better to die with a drink of some kind than to have none.

When his swollen tongue touched liquid, hope and strength sprang into Kean.

⁓

Two weeks later, they were still going, all alive, sick only from fatigue. Essa was out of the cockpit and doing her pitiful best to make the trailer go faster. There had been more incidences of the cacti and locating them was her real contribution.

The heat was less. There came the moment when they elected to travel by day.

Later, there were insects and larger life-forms. You can eat a scorpion if you can catch it. The team began to feel a slow swell of excitement, like a very small crowd awaiting a very big occasion. This was almost like normal living.

Nights later, the ground felt different under Kean's boots. There were blades of grass struggling through the sand. On the next morning, there was no doubt: the Big White had surrendered and was becoming a dry savannah where light breezes blew and bent the grasses.

When he heard the yelping of wild dogs, Kean stood taller, a man who felt confident of living a good few years yet.

The pack animals were wary, and it took Barb all her skill to shoot one. It was nothing like a charjaw; finer-featured and smaller, with a reddish tinge to its pelt. Tasted fine.

The first true waterhole was one more day's journey. They shared the joys of the muddy pool with a squirmation of colorful water snakes.

Now there were deer to be wondered at: large deer, big-eyed and round-bellied from good feed. The sun was nothing compared to that in the valley. The savannah rolled on and grew greener. Kean's clear eyes saw the green becoming richer still on the horizon.

He saw a dust cloud, too. Coming nearer.

Men, riding horses.

❦

They wore clothes of woven materials. Their horses stamped and fretted: incredible, high-strung beasts. Kean knew what they were without being told; he had heard tales of them often enough. The riders did not get within shouting distance of the trailer. They only paused to look, and then veered off on some mission elsewhere on the savannah, apparently incurious about the travelers.

There was a farm next. Only a small wooden building. The travelers passed it by because the farmer required them to—he very obviously wanted nothing to do with them. He was small and bearded, and wore the faded, lightweight clothes the riders affected. When he shouted at them, it was in a quick-fire voice, speaking a sibilant language they could not begin to understand.

Kean smiled courteously and they kept going. If the people here were not violent to them, he had no wish to make them so. "We don't know the rules here, and it looks like they don't speak our language. We got to be extra polite. We don't need anything from them, anyhow. We can live off the animals we hunt."

There were bizarrely tall trees with fresh leaves and shiny trunks, and more waterholes. The extraordinary joy of a day's calm rainfall pattering down.

The land began to rise up around them, forming hills proportioned much smaller than they were used to. Essa felt she could just sit and look and be happy.

Here the farms became bigger, and the farmhouses, too. The people were more prosperous—and ruder. The breathy, whispery language they spoke, or shouted, was hard to imitate even roughly; the sounds got caught in your throat. So far nobody had understood the words the three travelers spoke to them when they tried to communicate. The crops were not only grain—some were composed of green plants, too, with a glorious sheen on them. If you avoided the cultivated land, the farmers were content to let you pass through, after a little abuse. There was order here, and—

"Water," Essa said. She was hatless and looked healthy. Kean liked to look at her and did so now. She was smiling.

"We've got all the water we need," he told her.

"I know," she said, and smiled more.

⁓

Another hill to climb, in the comfortable morning sunshine. The grass so vividly green. A herd of wild horses off to their left; to their right a wide track, beaten down by use. They joined the track, pulling the trailer along it with ease.

A man and woman came by on a tall wooden cart drawn by bullocks, going the other way. They had a baby with them, a fat little despot enthroned on his mother's lap. The man smiled and chattered to them in a musical speech they had not heard before. The Wanderers grinned back and indicated their incomprehension, which earned them a more mistrustful goodbye from the family.

The team pulled on up the hill and breasted it, and there was the sea.

$\sim$

The verdant land tumbled down to where a sprawling town made of wood reached into the lazy gray-blue waters with jetties and walkways. There was no sandy beach; one moment there was dry land, and then a mangrove swamp confused the boundary between the water and the countryside.

The sea was big. You just knew it was bigger by far than the Big White, although it was not as empty. There were scores of tree-clad islands to be seen protruding from its depths, and a hundred little boats plied between them. The islands were all shapes and sizes, some relatively flat, others as sharp-featured as mountain peaks.

Farther out toward the horizon, there was only sea. Vast and still. The breeze from it had a tender touch.

Barb said, "That's . . . that's just . . ." and stopped.

Kean and Essa smiled at one another.

Looked at the sunlight playing on the distant water.

ACKNOWLEDGMENTS

For their part in *Wanderer*'s journey to the page, I must thank Carol Reyes of Cecily Ware Literary Agents for her faith in the book; Adam Newell of Titan Publishing for his advice on the American publishing scene; Laura Stiers for first pitching the novel and then editing it; and, as ever, my wife Joanna for her love and support. Finally, I thank Mary Chapin Carpenter for her album *Stones in the Road*, which I listened to constantly during the time I was writing *Wanderer*.